ARCHFIEND

PART III OF THE ANGEL CRUSH SAGA

BY

VIOLETTE L. MEIER

Viori Publishing
vioripublishing.com
Decatur, GA

Printed in the United States of America

Cover Designed by Viori Publishing

DEDICATED TO

…my family. You keep my dreams alive even when I lose sight of them. Thank you for seeing my vision even when my eyes are blurred.

…my loyal readers. Your support is my inspiration to create stories that I pray that you will always enjoy.

…Ari, the love of my life. You are my biggest fan and I am yours.

…my children. You are my everything.

ACKNOWLEDGEMENTS

Nothing is possible without God, my family, my friends, and my readers. Know that you are loved and appreciated in every way possible. Love you.

AUTHOR'S NOTE

Writing has been my first love since childhood, and I feel overwhelmingly honored that I am allowed the chance to share what circulates in my head daily. Imagination is the purest form of creation. In it, we are most like God; the masters and creators of worlds. Thank you for allowing me to share my stories. Within these pages, my sanity and sanctity battle for dominance. Sit back and enjoy the fight!

|

"I love you," Sadie whispered as she kissed her eldest son on the cheek; her metallic silver hair brushing against his face as he pulled away from her to stand up tall. When she looked up at his six feet four stature, it was hard to fathom that her baby was sixteen, a strikingly handsome young man; the spitting image of her late father, a high school graduate, was now being dropped off at college on a full academic and athletic scholarship. Where had the time gone? It was only yesterday when she found out that he was in her womb and fear and anticipation bubbled up within her. It seemed like soon after his birth, he left home for kindergarten, skipped up two grades because of his genius, came into his own, and wreaked havoc and destruction upon their entire family causing death after death, trouble after trouble, pain after pain.

A single tear fell from her left eye and traveled down her strangely youthful, but experienced face. She had the kind of unchanging beauty that caused people to marvel about her age. Sadie looked to be anywhere between twenty-six and forty years old. The best estimate depended upon what she was wearing at the time or the age revealing slang that she occasionally used.

"I love you too," Khalid responded smiling at his mother. He meant what he said, and he knew that she meant it too; although, the turbulence of their relationship caused them both great anguish. There were times he felt that she regretted the day he emerged from her womb, that she felt he was responsible for the death of her parents, and that his existence was the source of all her disenchantment. Despite it all, he loved her still and he was sure that she loved him unconditionally.

His father, for all practical purposes but not biological, James, the man who raised Khalid and loved him his whole life, and his brother Uriel stepped out of the car and stood before Khalid with proud and misty eyes.

"I'm gonna miss you," James said as he grabbed Khalid's hand and squeezed it so tight that Khalid thought that his bones would break and be forced out of his fingertips. "Do yo' work and stay outta trouble boy. Make yo mama proud. Here me?"

"Yes dad. Love you too," Khalid said as he looked into James's pitch-black face. James had lost so much weight over the years that his skin was pulled so tight around his skull that it was as if an invisible clamp was holding a meat ponytail behind his head causing his handsome face to look gaunt and hard. His bald head no longer needed to be shaved because his hair follicles no longer produced hair. Salt and pepper eyebrows framed his tired eyes which once were bright white but now a pastel yellow.

James pulled Khalid into a quick hug, stepped back, let go of Khalid's hand, then stepped aside so Uriel could say goodbye.

At fourteen years old and the spitting image of James, Uriel stood before his brother almost eye to eye. He stared deep into Khalid's eyes and felt himself being pulled into some dark dangling place on a distant side of the universe where dangerous things lurked waiting to feast upon souls. Uriel looked away, so reality could again take precedence, then turned back to face his big brother.

"I will miss you," Uriel admitted despite the ugliness he saw every time his gaze lingered too long on his brother's eyes. The darkness didn't matter. Uriel loved and liked his brother. "It won't be the same without you."

Khalid grabbed Uriel and pulled him into an embrace and said, "I will miss you too. Call me anytime and visit me sometimes. Take care of Mama and Daddy. Love you."

"Love you too," Uriel responded unable to release his arms from around his brother. Khalid was the peanut butter to his jelly.

"Let me go!" Khalid laughed as he poked Uriel in his ribs.

Uriel jumped back laughing while grabbing his side. "That hurt!" he howled.

"It was supposed to," Khalid quipped.

The Tucker family got back into their vehicle and waved goodbye as they disappeared down the road.

Uriel watched his brother walk away and fade behind a tall building.

Khalid was left amid a massive campus green with growth. Gray buildings sat on every other piece of land. The campus was large and beautiful with old buildings where great men passed through leaving remnants of their greatness for future generations to glean.

After a week, college was not what Khalid imagined. His mind shifted through images of nerds gathering on grass debating the universe, balding professors sitting cross-legged smoking cigars, cold classrooms that looked like amphitheaters, and dismissive antisocial females. Before he arrived, he imagined the campus would be infested with beautiful brown girls with full lips, round hips, and thirsty eyes drinking up every inch of him; party signs hanging above each dorm; and barking fraternity brothers stepping through the courtyard on hopping feet, twirling and tossing canes as they made the earth quake to the beat of their feet.

Khalid dropped the box he was holding onto the twin bed sitting against the right wall in a small dorm room. The painted stone walls looked sad next to a mattress wrapped in a houndstooth patterned sheet holding a box of belongings that should have been put in their respective places about a week ago.

It was cool, and the air conditioner hummed a muffled tune. Khalid looked across the room at his roommate's twin bed which was wrapped in a gray polka-dot sheet with a matching pillowcase and covered with a striped navy and gray comforter. A unique trio of posters picturing Marilyn Manson, Lil Wayne, and Katy Perry hung over his roommate's bed. A poster reading "Nirvana in Utero Tour" picturing Kurt Cobain with a man wearing angel wings behind him hung huge and alone at the head of the bed. The picture of the winged man reminded Khalid of his father. Every time he looked upon it, he felt that Turiel would descend from the heavens or whatever star he was trapped in to assure Khalid that he was still with him.

On the desk next to the bed, sat a laptop computer with a fruit engraved on its top and a stack of old dusty books that looked like they belonged in an ancient library long forgotten. There was also a wooden box with enigmatic markings sitting next to the computer with an old-fashioned keyhole in front of it. A cup of feather pens and a bottle of black ink sat next to the wooden box. Khalid thought, as he took inventory of his roommate's belongings, that Belial, his roommate, was very interesting indeed.

Khalid turned his attention back to the box on his bed and began to empty the contents one by one. Within no time, his empty desk was filled with paper, pens, and miscellaneous office supplies. A pack of ramen noodles and a box of cereal were placed on a small shelf above a miniature refrigerator, and a stack of towels were placed upon Khalid's dresser.

Khalid sat on his bed. Before he could lean back against his pillow and place his earbuds in his ears, Belial walked into the room with long gangling steps.

"Greetings," he said, his pale skin translucent with blue and purple veins making webs underneath. His clear blue eyes looked like dirty ice and a shadow of recently shaved short black hair peaked from the top of his head. He wore a plaid shirt with a crooked bowtie and pants that looked a size too small. He was short and slender with a pungent odor always floating from his mouth.

"What's up?" Khalid answered with a head nod, smelling Belial's insufferable breath from across the room.

"You, my friend," Belial said. "Always you."

Belial smiled a menacing smile and nodded. He moved across the room like a cat, silent and quick. His shadow lingered a few steps behind, even making a few moves out of sync with its master.

A chill ran down Khalid's back as he watched Belial and his shadow sit down at his desk and open his computer. Khalid placed his earbuds in and turned on his music hoping to drown out the ever-growing unease in the pit of his stomach.

II

The house seems empty without him, Sadie thought as she walked through the living room letting her fingers float across the top of the sofas. The subtle smell of Khalid –the scent of teen sweat, sport deodorant, and a tinge of myrrh so subtle only a mother's nose could detect, was still in the house. Sadie inhaled then flopped down on the couch. A part of her missed Khalid so much that she wanted to fall to the floor and weep. Another part of her wanted to get up, dance like it was 1999, and shout to God, the universe, Mother Nature or whomever was responsible for getting him out of their hair in exaltation. Since she couldn't figure out whether to bawl or boogie, she did nothing. Sadie allowed her head to fall back on the sofa pillows and her eyes to lock onto the plain, white, unmarked ceiling. Tears began to well up. She sighed. She missed him. Sadie couldn't help it. He was her first born son. How could she not?

"Baby," James called, as he walked into the living room breaking the thick silence, startling Sadie causing her to jump.

"Yes," she whispered, looking at James with glossy eyes. She blinked, and a fat tear rolled down her face. She wiped it away with the back of her hand.

Worry lines creased the sides of James's full lips.

Sadie secretly wondered if the stress of their family caused his handsomeness to wane. He looked so different from the gorgeous man she had married years ago. Not that he wasn't still attractive, but he looked ten years older than he was.

"You seen my gray basketball shorts? I put 'em in the laundry basket last week and I ain't seen 'em since," he said trying hard to ignore the mounting wetness of her eyes.

It was obvious that Sadie was missing Khalid. James missed him too, but truth be told, James was glad that Khalid was gone. Maybe with the boy gone, their home would have some sense of normality. Years of preternatural horrors were enough to last James for a lifetime. After Mrs. Covington died, Khalid went on a tirade of harmful behavior where a neighbor's child ended up paralyzed, three teachers died of mysterious causes, a few local churches were vandalized, and a lot of strange things reported by Uriel of Khalid levitating, eyes blackening, or chanting foreign words in his sleep. *Good riddance!* James thought. He had served his time as a devoted father to a child not his own; all for the love of Sadie. It was illogical to expect him to comfort her when they both should be celebrating Khalid's departure.

"I put them in your bottom drawer with your other basketball shorts," she sniffed as another tear escaped.

"Thanks, baby," answered James; bending to kiss her cheek, then quickly disappearing from the room.

Sadie let her head flop back and locked her eyes on the ceiling. Irritation with James replaced her mourning for Khalid. She wanted to jump up and chase James, so she could scream at him for his lack of concern, but she knew it would be no use. Arguing over the years had deflated them both to a point where they were limp weaklings trying hard just to hold on to any trace of passion they once shared. Their sixteen-year marriage had been the best and worst years of their lives; however, Sadie's optimism permitted her to believe that their relationship was not broken but bent.

Sadie picked up her cell phone and searched for Khalid's name. She texted *I love you* and a heart emoji; then placed the cell phone back on the table. A few seconds later, she received an emoji with heart shaped eyes back. Sadie smiled.

"James," Sadie called; her hands folded on her lap and her eyes squeezed tight. She needed him near her, needed to be in his arms. It was time.

"What up?" James answered sticking his head into the living room with his basketball shorts in hand. Fitted boxer shorts displayed his firm thighs, narrow hips, and an ample portion of manhood.

Sadie stood up from the couch and let her sundress hit the floor.

"Come here," she ordered, standing as naked as Eve.

James dropped his shorts to the floor, his eyes staring in utter disbelief. God had answered his prayers after almost a year of sexless relations with his wife. He obediently went to her and wrapped his arms around her tiny waist as his full lips found hers.

"I missed you, baby," he whispered as he kissed her deeply.

It had been eons since he had last held his wife. Sadie's mouth tasted like cotton candy. Her skin felt like a thousand feathers underneath his fingertips.

"I missed you too," she cooed as she hopped up and wrapped her legs around his waist. "Let's promise to never wait this long again."

James nodded, then slipped into her and began to rock her hips as he walked around the room. Buried deep within her thighs, he stroked hallelujah from her lips.

Into the crease of his neck, she suppressed her moans as they embraced a sliver of passion once again.

|||

The house was not the same without Khalid. Video games didn't seem as fun. Uriel found it hard to sleep without hearing Khalid whispering sweet nothings into his cell phone to the girl of the week. There was no one to double team James while playing weekend basketball, and there was no one to talk Sadie out of buying Uriel corny clothes that he would never wear. There was no one to argue over the last bowl of cereal or over whose turn it was to clean up the bathroom. Uriel really missed his big brother something awful. It was lonely without him.

It was getting late. Uriel got on his knees and said his prayers then languidly climbed into bed. The sound of his parents making love echoed through the house in symphonic moans. Uriel smiled. It had been a long time since he had heard them loving each other. It was painfully obvious that James and Sadie had been growing apart for years. Now, every coo from his mother and sigh from his father gave Uriel hope that their love was being renewed.

Secretly, Uriel feared that he would eventually become a product of divorce; that he would be one of those kids who lived in a different place during the summer and had to choose where he wanted to spend the holidays, but the racket they were making quieted those fears. It sounded like they were like they used to be.

Uriel picked up his cell phone, inserted his earphones, turned on his audio Bible, and allowed the overly dramatic voice of the reader to drown out the panting and sighs of his parents. The cadence of the reader's voice lulled him to sleep.

Gray. The world was gray. Khalid was the only flash of color in a grayscale universe. He walked over the earth with feet that crushed mountains into piles of dust. People squirmed to get out if his way; like roaches trying to evade the rain of bug spray. Then, black. Black arms and legs and torso with no ending or beginning followed behind Khalid as he marched across the earth. The shadow was upon his heels, then upon his back pulling him down onto the earth that crumbled beneath him. Khalid wrestled with the darkness, a flash of color and black until light pierced through and banished them both into nothingness.

Uriel's eyes popped open and he sat up in bed. His cell phone, which was lying on his chest, hit the floor pulling the earbuds from his ears. The strange dream caused his chest to tighten beneath his T-shirt. He took a deep breath and shook his head free of the images that worried his mind. Uriel grabbed his cell phone from the floor and swiped the screen until a picture of his brother appeared. He hit the call button and waited as the phone rang in his ear.

"Hello," Khalid's voice cracked as he fought himself free of sleep.

"Hey Lid," Uriel said while propping his pillows against his headboard and leaning back. His heart was still drumming within his chest and his hands were trembling.

"What up?" Khalid grumbled, the time on his phone read: 3:33 am. "Why are you calling so late?"

"I had a bad dream about you," Uriel said trying to calm down before he finished speaking.

"Dude, I have class in the morning," Khalid grumbled. "Out with it so I can go back to sleep!" Khalid said irritably. He thought the days of Uriel waking him up to tell him about dreams were over. Obviously, Khalid was wrong.

"You were wrestling with a shadow" Uriel spat, "and you both disappeared."

"And what else?" Khalid asked totally uninterested in what Uriel was saying. Dreamland was his only desire; dreamland and the copper colored girl sound asleep under his armpit.

"Nothing else," Uriel sighed. "Sorry I woke you."

"Talk to you later," Khalid huffed. "Love you, bro," he mumbled under his breath and hung up the phone.

"Love you too," Uriel responded into a silent phone. He tossed the phone onto his nightstand and closed his eyes. He contemplated telling his parents, but he didn't want to cause them to worry. They had enough to worry about. It would be hours before he would calm his nerves enough to go to sleep.

IV

It was getting cool in New York City, but it was always warm in Dr. and Mrs. Cohen's upper eastside apartment. The heat was turned up to a cozy seventy-eight degrees. The enormous apartment was quiet at that late hour. Jupiter, Venus, Earth, and Mars Cohen rested in their respective bedrooms as their parents splashed around in the shower of their master bathroom.

Bubbles covered Sky from neck to toe as she soaped up in the shower next to her equally soapy husband. Forrest picked up the soap and ran his fingers over her breast as the shower water distorted her giggles and ran into her mouth.

"Time for your breast exam," Forrest joked as he cupped one of her breasts while kissing her bottom lip.

"Yes Dr. Cohen," Sky obliged by putting her hands behind her head and poking her chest out; her scarlet spirals of hair straightened under the pounding water.

Forrest caressed her left breast, stopping only to admire her reddish-brown areolas. He moved excitedly to the right one, but first decided to tickle her armpit. Sky giggled, but Forrest's smile suddenly turned upside down. His fingers went from fondling to aggressively examining.

"What's wrong?" Sky asked, her giggle fading into the raining shower water.

"There's a hard lump in your armpit," he answered while taking her hand and placing her fingers upon it. "Do you feel it?" Forrest asked.

"It's nothing," Sadie replied. "That's been there for years."

"What?" Forrest asked, baffled that he had never discovered it. "Does it hurt?"

"Sometimes," she admitted. "But not really. I just figured it was a swollen gland or something. My mama said I always had swollen glands. When I get sick, I get knots on my neck. I figured my deodorant was stopping up a musk gland or something. You know how I be sweatin'" Sky laughed.

"Sky, why haven't you mentioned this before? This could be serious!" Forrest spat.

He turned off the water and pulled down a towel and began to dry his wife off.

"I will make you an appointment immediately with Dr. Regina Izan," said Forrest as he wrapped the towel around her; then, began to dry himself. "She is the best doctor in New York."

"I thought you were the best doctor in New York," Sky jibbed.

"This is serious Sky," he scolded. "I can't believe you didn't tell me about that thing in your armpit. You usually tell me everything."

"Don't go blowing things out of proportion. It's not that serious," Sky whined, kissing his neck as he buffed his back. "If I felt like something was wrong, I would have told you and I would have asked my doctor about it."

"This is not up for debate. You will see Dr. Izan this week. I will make sure of that," Forrest demanded.

"Okay," Sky smirked. She found it sexy how much he worried about her. She found it even sexier when he put a little bass in his voice when he tried to tell her what to do. "I'll go."

"You better," Forrest grumbled angrily. "You of all people should know better! I'm a doctor Sky. You shouldn't be self-diagnosing on Google like you have no health insurance!"

Sky crossed her arms and cut her eyes.

"I get the point," she snapped. "I said that I will go see Dr. Izan. Can we change the subject now?"

"No, we can't change the subject!" Forrest belched and threw his towel over the shower rod. "I want you to take your health seriously. We depend on you to take care of yourself and our family."

"Don't you think you are blowing this out of proportion?" Sky asked, following him out of the bathroom into the bedroom.

Forrest climbed into the bed and pulled the covers over his slightly damp body, and held up the other side of the comforter for Sky to climb in. She folded her towel and laid it on the purple fainting couch at the foot of their bed, then climbed into the bed into the crux of Forrest's armpit.

"Promise me you will not miss the appointment I set," said Forrest with a kiss to her forehead.

Sky promised as she wrapped her arms around his chest and wondered why her husband's worry for her was so intense. It was just a small lump. It really wasn't that serious.

V

Classes were a breeze, and Khalid was getting more bored with college each day. He had quickly become the cool guy on campus. Everyone wanted him at their parties. The hottest girls competed to get next to him. Professors gloated on his genius. All the fraternities bombarded him with invitations. The swim team lauded him for winning first place in all their meets. Khalid wished he could just test out of school and graduate immediately, but he knew his parents wanted him to enjoy the college experience of a HBCU, and truly network. He couldn't count how many times he had heard his father tell him that it is who you know not what you know. Fundamentally, Khalid knew that was true for most people, but he was not most people. He had the power of persuasion. There weren't many people alive who he could not get to do what he wanted them to do. Persuasion was a natural gift for him. Some people could sing. Some people could compute numbers faster than a computer. Some people could sculpt figures so lifelike that they seemed to draw breath. Khalid could manipulate any situation to benefit him. That was his gift, to lead and control the masses. People loved him. They lingered on his every word. They followed him aimlessly. He was well liked and loved by everyone he met; everyone except for his roommate Belial.

Belial was a strange fellow. Every time Khalid's gaze met Belial's eyes, it was like a force field formed between them. None of Khalid's charms worked on the odd boy. Belial met each of Khalid's requests with an unapologetic no and went on about his business. This bugged Khalid. He could not understand what strange power Belial possessed.

Khalid's sixteen years of wisdom had taught him that there was no such thing as coincidence. Everything was a part of a grand scheme. Therefore, there was a reason, sinister or divine, that Belial had crossed his path.

"Good evening," Belial greeted, the smell of Belial's breath breaking Khalid's train of thought.

Khalid looked up from his desk at the yellow toothed smile of Belial. His teeth were like pats of butter or maybe artificially colored margarine.

Belial's pale translucent skin reminded Khalid of Danny DeVito's portrayal of The Penguin in one of those corny 90s Batman movies that his dad made him and Uriel watch when they were kids.

"Good evening," Khalid responded. An uneasy feeling snaked down his spine as he considered his roommate's insipid eyes. The unease harnessed a bit of excitement for Khalid. He pulled a pack of gum from his pocket; offering a piece to Belial with hopes that he would accept it and the room would be momentarily free from the stench of his breath. But to Khalid's dismay, Belial declined with a wave of his hand.

Belial moved quickly towards his bed, his shadow making a few movements contrary to its owner, and placed his books down.

"How was your day?" Belial asked in a voice that sounded ancient and educated in the finest institutions in the world. "By the look in your eyes, it was quite a bore."

"Very boring," Khalid responded finding it difficult to draw his eyes away from the shadow sitting in a totally different position than Belial.

"Let me know when you are ready for some real excitement. I have some things in my box," Belial pointed to the chest sitting upon his desk, "that you may find satisfactory."

Khalid stared at the dusty chest covered in ancient script. It was true that the box peaked his interest, but an ache in the pit of his gut prevented him from quenching his curiosity.

"I got too much homework to do," Khalid said trying hard to pull his eyes away from the box. Something inside of the chest was calling for him. He felt the call deep within his being like a mental whispering that would not cease.

Belial let out a high-pitched laugh that tore Khalid's eyes from the chest and locked them on his cackling roommate.

"Another time my friend. Another time," Belial laughed as Khalid turned back to his desk and damned himself for not putting in a request for a new roommate.

VI

"Which mathematical equation is referred to as the most beautiful equation and why?" an old pink skinned professor asked as he paced across the lecture room with his arms folded behind his back. The sound of his curled-at-the-toe shoes echoed through the room.

"Friedmann's equation," a young woman blurted out full of confidence. "It is the most beautiful equation."

"Loud and wrong as usual, Miss Hall. It seems to me that you should become weary of being incorrect by now. It can't be great for your self-esteem," the professor blurted in a monotone voice.

The class laughed.

"Would your boyfriend Mr. Tucker like to answer?" the professor asked.

Khalid smiled at his sulking girlfriend. He patted her knee to nudge away her embarrassment, and answered, "Euler's Identity is known as The Beautiful Equation."

"Can you explain to Miss Yvette Hall why?" the professor asked. "She seems to linger on every word you say. Maybe you can impart some knowledge to her since she apparently has no ability to retain any from me."

The class laughed again.

Yvette crossed her arms and pouted.

"The equation links together the most important symbols in math (0, 1, i, pi, and e), algebra, and geometry," Khalid answered the professor and playfully popped Yvette's thigh bringing a smiled to her pouting face.

"You are right Mr. Tucker. Now, if only you can rub some of your brilliance on your playmate, you two will be a force to be reckoned with! Class dismissed." The professor waved his hand and disappeared out of the back door.

"I hate him!" Yvette sneered as she picked up her books and followed Khalid out of the classroom. "That fat bastard has the nerve to tell you to rub some brilliance off on me like I'm dumb or somethin'. I may not have graduated the top of my class, but my test scores were a point from perfect!" Yvette smacked her thick, glossy lips and rolled her eyes. "Next time he say somethin' smart, Imma slap them crooked glasses off his fat face. Old pimple face punk!"

Khalid laughed hysterically. He loved her around-the-way-girl attitude. The way she smacked her big lips and rolled her almond eyes turned him on. Blonde braids touched her down-south, one hundred percent natural ghetto booty, making an interesting contrast with her copper skin as they swung when she walked.

"Have you noticed that he always has something demeaning to say about women?" Yvette complained. "Especially me! I think he hates me or somethin'. He calls me Two Points."

"Why?" Khalid asked.

"Because he told me I was two IQ points away from being a rock," she spat.

Khalid laughed hysterically.

"It's not funny. He just don't like me. One time I went to his office to ask him a question and he closed the door in my face and said that he was not taking any more appointments, but he let the boy that was waitin' behind me in."

"He's old and sexist. It is what it is," Khalid retorted. "The best way to shut him up is to be the best. When you are the best, no one can argue with that."

"I guess. But why he always gotta pick on me?" she whined. Being old and sexist was not a valid excuse for being a horrible person she thought. That was like excusing someone for being racist just because that was the way they were taught. Yvette concluded that the professor's problem was that too many people excused his bad behavior which allowed him to become more ridiculous over the years.

"Ignore him. Perhaps he wants you for himself," Khalid answered. "You are fine as hell. He probably has never seen a booty as big as yours in real life. You're like walking porn!"

"Whatever!" Yvette grinned. It was flattering to think that the old man may have been secretly lusting after her. "Wanna get something to eat?"

"Yep, after you gimme some of yo cookies," Khalid mocked her stereotypical inner-city accent and grabbed her behind.

Yvette giggled. She said, "I can't. I got class in thirty minutes!" and popped his fondling hand.

"All I need is ten," Khalid pulled her close and kissed her on the neck. Before his lips could reach her ear, his eyes caught the eyes of a beautiful ebony skinned woman standing behind Yvette. He pulled back and said to Yvette while locking eyes with the other woman, "If you're busy, baby, I understand."

Khalid smiled and licked his lips. He ravished her with his eyes. The woman smiled back and bit her finger.

Puzzled by his sudden change of demeanor, Yvette turned around and saw the grinning girl that she had caught Khalid sleeping with the week before. Last week, Yvette decided to surprise Khalid with a picnic, but walked into a surprise of her own. When she entered his dorm room without knocking, she caught a naked Khalid thrusting behind the grinning girl with her skirt hiked up around her waist and both howling like dogs in heat. Yvette threw the picnic basket at them and ran away. A few days later, Khalid called her to apologize and took her to dinner and a movie. She instantly forgave him.

Yvette gave the young woman the middle finger and mouthed a derogatory insult. She turned to Khalid with anger and hurt in her eyes.

"You still messin' wit' her?" Yvette's voice trembled. Her fist balled, and she started to breathe rapidly. "Tell me the truth!"

"Naw," Khalid laughed, ignoring her emotional pain.

Yvette turned to the other woman and yelled, "Don't make me slap the taste out of your mouth. Keep your eyes off my man you grimy ho! Next time I won't be so nice!"

The girl laughed, completely unafraid, and winked at Khalid. She put her pinky and thumb to the side off her face and mouthed, "Call me."

"Let's go!" Yvette growled, not taking her eyes off the other woman. Yvette gave the other woman the middle finger again then grabbed Khalid by his collar and pulled him toward his dorm room.

"I thought you had class," Khalid laughed stumbling over his feet as she pulled him like a mother would pull a tantrum throwing child out of a mall.

"Forget class! Imma whip it on you until I'm the only woman you will ever see!" she spat marching across the campus as if she was going to war.

VII

Dr. Regina Izan was the best women's health doctor in New York City. Women sang her praises from New York to as far as Washington, D.C. They lauded her intermingling of natural medicine and traditional Western medicine. It was likely that she would write a prescription for ginger and cayenne pepper, before a pharmaceutical drug. She was in such high demand that it was easier to get an appointment with the President of the United States than it was to get an appointment with Dr. Izan; therefore, Sky was very fortunate that Dr. Izan was a friend of her husband.

"Sky Cohen," an Asian woman with a small voice called from behind a large circular desk. Her bobbed raven hair was held by two silver barrettes, and her name tag read, *Mai*.

Sky, who was sitting cross legged in a comfortable waiting room chair, looked up from her magazine. She closed the magazine and turned to her husband who was sitting next to her scrolling the internet on his phone.

"Did she call me?" she asked.

"Yep," Forrest answered, dimming the screen on his cell phone and putting it into his pocket.

The couple stood up, joined hands, and walked over to the desk.

"Dr. Izan will see you now. Go through the double doors and enter room six. She will be with you in a moment," the receptionist instructed. She turned to Forrest and said, "You may wait for your wife out here."

"Naw. He goin' wit me!" Sky snapped and grabbed her husband's hand and pulled him inside the door.

Forrest laughed.

The receptionist rolled her eyes as they walked inside the door.

He mouthed to the receptionist, *She's just nervous. I'm sorry* and followed quickly behind his wife.

"Why must you be so dramatic?" Forrest asked as they walked into a room with a giant green 6 hanging on the door.

"That's what I do!" Sky retorted, dropping her purse on the examining table and sitting down on the doctor's stool.

"Are you nervous sweetheart?" Forrest asked. "You're acting a little bit crazy." He folded his arms and leaned against the wall.

Her kinky red hair was pinned up in the back but fell over her right eye in a puffy swoop. Scarlet freckles danced across her golden red cheeks as she sat with her green eyes blazing and her ruby lips twisted to the side. After almost two decades, Sky was still the most exquisite woman Forrest had ever seen.

"Why would I be nervous? I know my body. I'm fine," Sky retorted, suddenly avoiding his eyes which made Forrest even more nervous because he could see that his wife was not as confident as she pretended.

They continued in silence for about fifteen minutes before a short ebony skinned woman walked into the door. Her short natural hair was standing up all over her head in auburn twists. The doctor's hair reminded Sky of her favorite barbeque twist chips. The doctor's kind smile stretched across her face like an upside-down rainbow.

Forrest walked over to the woman and pulled her in for a hug. She happily accepted amid light hearted laughter.

"Regina, it's so good to see you," Forrest exclaimed as he kissed her smooth black cheek. "You haven't aged a day."

"It's good to see you too. Too many years!" Dr. Regina Izan replied. "I think the last time I saw you was when we worked together in India."

"Aw, it hasn't been that long!" Forrest laughed. "We saw each other in passing at a fundraising benefit about seven years ago."

"You are right. It was a benefit for inner city children. I remember!" she replied. "Still, it has been nearly a decade. What a shame."

Sky faked a cough.

Forrest let go of the doctor and said, "This is my wife Sky, and the reason for our visit."

Dr. Izan pulled Sky up from the stool and locked her in the kind of hug that a grandmother would give. The short woman only reached Sky's chest. The side of her small face pressed into Sky's ribs. Sky gasped for air then let out a hearty laugh.

"It is so wonderful to meet you!" Dr. Izan laughed. "You are the prettiest red thing that I have seen in my whole life!"

"Thank you," Sky laughed. "And you are just beautiful. I usually don't allow Forrest to be friends with gorgeous women," Sky joked.

It was true. The doctor was beautiful, but Sky knew that she was and would always be the apple of her husband's eye.

"Honey I try!" Dr. Izan exclaimed. "They say black don't crack, but when you get to be my age, you start seeing cracks everywhere."

"Your age? You couldn't be more than forty," Sky said curiously.

Dr. Izan's skin was smooth and tight, her body fit, and her energy youthful.

"I wish," the doctor said, letting Sky go and stealing her stool away from Sky. "I am sixty-two."

"How could that be?" Sky said aloud, truly astounded by the doctor's youthful beauty.

"Clean living honey. I keep my prayer life intact to make sure my most important relationship, with God, is maintained. I married a man who adores me, and we have been happy for twenty-five years. The second time was the charm. It was the third time for him. Honey, if at first you don't succeed, try and try again. You two were lucky to get it right the first time!" The doctor laughed.

She continued, "No drugs, no alcohol, no cigarettes, and very little junk food. I drink plenty of water and laugh like a fool as much as I can. I walk every day and dance twice a week. I don't believe in plastic surgery unless you have been maimed or born with a defect. I don't believe in body girdles. My husband likes all my jiggle as long as it is in the right places!" she laughed aloud again. "I teach my patients to pay attention to their bodies. No one should know your body better than you. So, the long and the short of it, I take care of myself and you should too," Dr. Izan imparted.

"You are truly gorgeous," Sky complimented, still wheeling from the doctor's age. "How did you and Forrest meet?"

"I was his supervisor overseas. He was a young doctor ready to heal the world, and I taught him that true healing was not just through medicine, but through food, exercise, clean living, and the earth. Honey, God gave us everything we need naturally to take care of our bodies. But, there are some things a little cayenne pepper can't cure, that's when we have to take a more aggressive approach to medicine."

Sky listened astutely.

"Now, what brings you here?" Dr. Izan's voice switched from jovial to serious.

"Sky has a...," Forrest was cut short by a wave of the doctor's finger.

"I'm sure Mrs. Sky has no problem speaking for herself," Dr. Izan said. "I like to tap the source."

"I apologize Regina," Forrest smiled timidly. Sometimes talking to her felt like talking to his mother. Her voice was soft, but kind of intimidating.

"Sit on the examining table sweetheart. Forrest, push over that stepping stool. I need some height for this tall drink of water," the doctor directed.

Sky sat upon the examining table and handed her purse to Forrest.

"I have a large lump in my armpit, and a few small ones in my breast," Sky admitted.

Forrest's eyes stretched wide. He had no knowledge of the lumps in her breast.

The doctor observed Forrest's reaction and asked Sky, "Would you be more comfortable without your husband in the room?"

"Oh no," Sky answered. "There is nothing I can say to you that I cannot say in front of him."

"Very well," Dr. Izan said. "How long has the lumps been there?

"For years. I just thought that the lump under my arm was an allergic reaction to my deodorant. My skin can be very sensitive at times, so I didn't think much of it. The ones in my breast are relatively new. Recently they have been a little painful," Sky replied.

"Why didn't you tell me?" Forrest asked, his expression mixed with disbelief and hurt.

"I didn't think it was a big deal. Baby, I'm sorry," Sky apologized. "I thought it was probably the underwire in my bras that was causing the discomfort."

"There you go with all that self-diagnosis again," Forrest huffed.

Dr. Izan gave Forrest the side eye. He leaned back and stopped talking. His face reflected his displeasure.

"Remove your blouse so I can examine you," the doctor instructed.

Sky did as she was told, and the doctor pushed her cold hands into Sky's armpit.

Sky winced.

"Please remove your bra," Dr. Izan said.

Sky removed her bra, and the doctor ran her fingers across Sky's freckled breasts; gently kneading and cupping the flesh searching for abnormal lumps.

"You may put your shirt back on," Dr. Izan said with a hint of concern in her eyes.

Sky put back on her blouse and waited for the doctor to speak.

"What did your doctor say?" Dr. Izan asked Sky.

"I didn't tell my doctor," Sky admitted. "I truly didn't think anything was wrong."

"When was your last complete exam?" Dr. Izan asked.

"I get an examination every year," answered Sky.

"And your doctor didn't feel anything?" Dr. Izan asked with a tiny bit of anger in her voice.

Sky answered, "I guess not."

"Unacceptable! He or she should have noticed these lumps long ago." Dr. Izan exclaimed. She shook her head. "I suggest that you find a more qualified doctor. One that cares about the health of their patients! A matter of fact, if you would have me, I would like to be your new doctor."

"Thank you," Sky said.

"Is everything okay?" Forrest interjected.

"I am ordering a full examination and a biopsy," Dr. Izan said. "Then I will be able to answer your question more accurately."

Sky's heartbeat quickened. Her nervousness turned to fear.

"I want to see you back in my office this week. I will ensure that Mai schedules you immediately," Dr. Izan smiled weakly. She kissed Sky on the cheek and said, "It was such a pleasure to meet you honey. Know that you are in good hands."

"It was a pleasure to meet you too," Sky responded as she hopped down from the examining table.

"Forrest, I enjoyed seeing you. I am so proud that you have grown to be such a phenomenal physician. Your reputation precedes you. Rest assured that I will provide your lovely wife with the best care that I can possibly give her."

"I know you will Regina. That is why I brought her to you. There is no one that I trust more," Forrest responded.

"I will see you very soon," Dr. Izan said to Sky. "Check with the receptionist about your next appointment. Enjoy the rest of your day."

"We will," Sky and Forrest said in unison as they walked out of the examining room.

After the door was closed, Dr. Izan sat on her stool and scribbled onto her notepad. Sadness descended upon her as she wrote. The thought of her dear friend Forrest possibly losing someone he loved broke her heart.

VIII

As usual, Professor Donovan was being a royal pain. Every time Khalid walked into the professor's classroom, it was as if the man focused all his hate, disgust, and contempt towards Khalid's girlfriend Yvette. No matter what she did, how many questions she answered correctly, how she excelled in her studies, Professor Donovan had something negative to say to her or about her. Yvette was the butt of every one of his jokes. He said something snide after all her responses. He made fun of her "inner-city" background, her bright blonde braids, and her around-the-way dialect. Lord forbad she answered a question wrong; he never gave up an opportunity to humiliate her in front of the class. It seemed as if his entire purpose in life was to make her angry, and Khalid was getting very weary of the professor's bullying.

Professor Donavan scribbled on the blackboard, his back to the class. The sound of the scratching chalk hovered in the background of Khalid and Yvette's conversation. The two spoke a tad above a whisper as they leaned across their desks.

"Can I come over tonight?" Yvette asked popping gum between words. Her round behind hung off the side of the seat as she sat on one hip trying to lean closer to Khalid.

"We'll see. I got homework to do," Khalid answered with a smirk on his face. "You're a distraction." His eyes drank in her thick legs and juicy lips.

"I promise we'll actually study this time," she giggled a little too loud causing Professor Donavan to spin around on his heels. His eyes narrowed and zoomed into Yvette's mentally exasperated face.

"Miss Hall, what's so funny?" his wrinkled eyes were vindictive slits like those of a serpent waiting patiently to bite the flute player who kept tempting him from a basket.

Yvette turned away from Khalid and faced the hissing instructor.

"Nothing sir," she answered.

Yvette straightened up; her feet flat on the floor. She damned herself for provoking the professor again. Just twenty minutes before, he had gone on a rant about her insufferable accent.

"No need to lie. You squealed like pork in a skirt. Please share with the class what delighted you so." He crossed his arms and waited.

"Khalid and I were having a personal conversation. I'm sorry if I disturbed the class," Yvette apologized.

"We all know that you are sorry Ms. Hall. Your work in my class reflects that," Professor Donovan barked. "I don't appreciate…"

"Lay off," Khalid said, his eyes narrowing and darkening.

"Pardon me?" the professor asked, surprised by Khalid's rebuttal.

"Leave her alone. She apologized, so move on," Khalid said. "I won't tell you again."

A big grin stretched across Yvette's face.

"Mr. Tucker, contrary to popular belief, this is my class. I am the authority here," the professor hissed. "You can let the door hit you on the way out right behind your homegirl!"

"Sir, there is no need for you to be disrespectful. Day after day you strive to humiliate her in front of the class. She should have reported you to the Dean long ago," Khalid replied.

The professor laughed. He wasn't worried about anyone reporting him to the Dean. The Dean was his brother. His family was one of the university's founding members. Long time donations and tenure secured the professor's employment for a lifetime.

Khalid leaned forward, his eyes swirling pools of blackness.

The professor grabbed his chest with a short breathless moan.

"Apologize to her," Khalid demanded, his lips curling into a sinister snarl, his blacked-out eyes affixed to the professor's.

"Never," the professor coughed as the left side of his body went numb. He tried to avert his eyes, but they remained locked with Khalid's shadowy eyes. One side of the professor's mouth twisted downward into a crooked drooling hole. His left arm and fingers bent and folded into something that resembled the short limb of a Tyrannosaurus Rex.

A girl on the front row of the class screamed as the man curled into a crippled ball. Another student called 911 as Khalid pulled Yvette up from her chair and ran out of the classroom.

|X

Sky sat on her living room couch with tears moistening her emerald eyes. Days before, she had received her results from an MRI, and the results were not good. Next thing she knew, she was staring at the ceiling as Dr. Izan inserted a long needle into her breast and armpit taking tissue samples to test for cancer cells. Now, all Sky had to do was wait; wait for life or wait for death. Come what may, just let the wait be over.

"Mama, your phone is ringing," Sky's youngest daughter Earth said as she skipped into the room with her massive red hair bouncing like a bloody cloud and handed the buzzing cell phone to her mother.

Earth looked identical to Sky from the wild green eyes to the red freckled skin. The young teen was not as slender as her mother, but very thin nonetheless. She had a little curve to her straightness.

"Thank you, baby," Sky said as she swiped the screen to answer.

"Mrs. Cohen?" Dr. Izan asked.

"Yes," Sky answered. "Hold for a moment," she said and pulled the phone away from her ear. "This is a personal call," she told Earth. "Give me some privacy."

"Okay Ma," Earth said as she walked away slowly. Something in the air did not feel right. Everything in her spirit told her to stay put, but she did not want to face the wrath of Sky, so she obediently left the room.

"Yes," Sky said into the phone. "How can I help you?"

"This is Dr. Izan. How are you today?" the doctor inquired.

"I'm okay. And you?" Sky asked.

She hated small talk. She wanted to yell *Get to it!* but, she was raised to respect her elders. The sound of the doctor's voice made Sky uneasy.

"I do fair for a square," the doctor answered. "Is your husband home?"

"Not yet," Sky answered.

The doctor's friendly procrastination graded against Sky's nerves. If the doctor didn't get to the point of the call soon, Sky was going to start cussing.

Dr. Izan said, "I have your test results. Would you like to wait for Forrest or..."

"Give it to me straight doc. I don't have the kind of patience to beat around the bush," Sky admitted. "No disrespect, but I can't wait another minute."

"None taken sweetheart," Dr. Izan said. "I prefer to discuss this in person."

"The phone is just fine," snapped Sky.

"Are you sure?" Dr. Izan asked. "I would rather for you to come to my office or maybe meet for lunch."

"Spit it out!" Sky spat.

The doctor cleared her throat and said, "I am very sorry to inform you that you have stage four breast cancer. The metastatic tumor has spread to your lungs, lymph nodes, and nearby organs. I recommend that we start chemotherapy immediately and immunotherapies soon after as a secondary tactic."

Sky dropped the phone on the floor. She felt like she had been hit in the face with a metal rod. She fell back on the sofa and squeezed her eyes shut. The thought of not seeing her four children grow into adulthood tore her soul right out of her body. The thought of her husband mourning her, like her father mourned over her mother, drove her soul out of the very room.

"Sky," the doctor called through the phone. "Sky!" The doctor repeated several times before disconnecting the call. She called again and got no answer.

Sky sat on the sofa with her eyes squeezed shut for about thirty minutes before her sixteen-year-old son Jupiter and her eight-year-old son Mars walked into the living room dribbling a basketball. The bouncing ball, to Sky, was the equivalent of a religious zealot knocking on her door at 7:00 am on a Saturday morning after a late Friday night. Her red rimmed eyes popped open.

"What did I tell you boys about playin' in the house?" Sky hissed, trying hard to stop a guttural bawl from escaping her trembling lips. Tears streamed down her face. She wiped them quickly with the back of her hand so fast that she scratched her face with her wedding ring.

"Don't cry. We wasn't playin' Mama," Mars said, his light brown skin glowing with sweat and his curly black hair reflecting the lamp light. Sincerity glistened in his dark green eyes. He looked more like Forrest than all the other children. He was the biracial version of his father.

"I was coming to ask you if I could take Mars to the basketball court with me," Jupiter said, his voice almost as deep as his father's. He looked like a male version of his mother, tall, thin, and red. Reddish brown cornrows held together with black rubber bands shaped his head. He wore a Malcolm X t-shirt with an ankh around his neck.

"Go ahead," Sky whispered.

"You a'ight?" Jupiter asked, handing the ball to his little brother and sitting next to her on the sofa. "What's wrong?"

Sky wept uncontrollably. Her moans echoed through the house.

"Ma!" Jupiter called, alarmed by his mother's cries. He had never seen his mother cry. Her tears frightened him beyond comprehension. "Why you cryin'? What happened?"

The sound of Sky's mewling forced fourteen-year-old Earth and fifteen-year-old Venus out of the kitchen.

Venus ran to her mother, her long black hair falling down her back in thick waves. Her brown skin and face reflected the beauty of her Nigerian grandmother.

"Mama!" Venus wailed. "What's wrong?"

All four children surrounded Sky on the sofa, limbs wrapped around her like noodles. They rocked her as she cried and they all cried as well not knowing the source of her pain. They hurt because she hurt. They wept because she wept. They howled because she howled until the front door opened minutes later.

Forrest walked into the house. To his horror, his entire family was balled up on the sofa crying like babies.

"What's going on?" he asked leaving the door wide open and rushing over to his wife and children. "What's going on Sky?"

She looked up at him, her eyes hopeless green puddles. Instantly he knew.

"Did you tell the kids?" he asked.

"No," she whispered.

"Tell us what?" Jupiter asked; his deep voice rumbling through the room.

Earth looked at her mother then over her mother's shoulder. Standing behind her was a dark-skinned woman wearing traditional African garb. Earth blinked. The woman smiled at Earth then disappeared. Earth buried her head in her mother's shoulder.

"Ma?" Venus asked, her heart palpitating. "Talk to us."

Mars climbed into his mother's lap and rubbed the side of her face. "Don't cry Mama," he said. "Everything is gonna be alright. Grandma was just behind you and she smiled," he confessed innocently.

Sky and Forrest looked at each other in utter surprise.

Sky's mother had passed long before her children were born. They had only known her through Sky's memories and photo albums.

Earth lifted her head. She turned to her little brother.

"You saw her?" Earth asked.

"Yes," Mars answered.

"Me too," Earth whispered.

"Enough of the ghost stories!" Venus screamed, her hands balled up. "What's wrong Mama? Why are you crying?"

"Sit down," Sky said. She wiped her eyes and made room for everyone on the sofa.

Forrest sat on the coffee table in front of them.

"I want you all to know that I love you so much," Sky said. "There isn't a day that I don't thank God for each of you. You have made my life beautiful. Each one of you hold a very special place in my heart."

"We love you too," Earth said.

"Shut up! Let her finish," Venus snapped.

"You shut up," Earth whispered.

"You both be quiet and listen!" Forrest growled. "If I hear a peep out of either one of you, you both will be grounded for infinity."

Venus rolled her eyes and Earth buried her face into her mother's arm, but neither said another word.

Sky stood up and moved near her husband, so she could face her children. She sat across his lap, her long legs draping him like a blanket. She wrapped her arm around his neck and cleared her throat.

"Today I was diagnosed with stage four cancer," she said, her eyes moving from one child to another. "I am sorry for not holding myself together, but I want to make it clear that I will be okay. I will fight this."

One by one the children began to weep until their voices became a chorus of lament. Tears ran down Forrest's face as he kissed his wife's neck and their children gathered around them both in a force field of love.

X

For the first time in years, a matter of fact, for the first time in their marriage, Sadie and James felt like newlyweds. This was the first time that they had a chance to focus solely on each other. They took long walks in the evenings, held hands in the car, ate off the same plate, and made love every night. It was like it was when they first started dating; before the turmoil's that neither of them could imagine would occur; before stresses, deaths, broken relationships, fear, and confusion set in to strain their sacred bond.

From the beginning, their marriage was turbulent because of the paranormal nature of their oldest son Khalid. Since his birth, their lives alternated between chaos and disorder. People close to them perished. Constant trauma drove them to the brink of insanity. Now, there was finally peace. Since Khalid had been away at school, they enjoyed an almost worry-free normal life.

Hot days followed by steamy nights gave the couple a true revival. They were free to enjoy each other thanks to Uriel's independent nature. The fourteen-year-old kept himself busy with books, video games, and school work as his parents found time in their schedules to date.

Uriel was happy for his parents. Seeing them in love made him feel more secure about their family. For years, he and Khalid feared that their parents would divorce. Many times, they wished it because of the emotional coldness between the two would become unbearable. The way they cordially patronized each other was sickening. Every night

Uriel prayed for their relationship's renewal and God had finally answered that prayer.

It was almost midnight and the Tuckers had not returned from dinner. It was a Friday night, so Uriel decided to stay up and play video games with his friends online. That lasted for a few hours before Uriel became bored of beating them, so he turned off his video game system and decided to watch TV. As usual, nothing caught his attention, so he turned it off and picked up a book. He read until he got tired. He closed his book and began his evening meditation. Uriel looked at the clock and time seemed to not have moved. So, after eating a bowl of cereal and talking to Khalid on the phone for fifteen minutes, Uriel decided to go to bed.

Sleep was unpleasant. Uriel tossed and turned as he tried to fight away thoughts of Sky. He dreamed of her as a skeleton; as dry bones dressed in bohemian garb. Frizzy hair covered her skull. Green eyes suspended in nothingness rolled around in her sockets. Gold and silver rings decorated the bones of her fingers and toes. Forrest clung to her legs, threatening to pull them apart at the joints. Her children danced around her in cloaks of black; caped shadows spinning like ballerinas. Uriel wept with them. His cries joined theirs in a wave of sobs. Uriel walked toward her, reaching out his hand until they were flesh to bone. He touched her hand and her dry bones started to shine. Patches of flesh appeared on the bone.

"Uriel!" Someone shook his shoulder waking him from his sleep. "Wake up, baby. It's just a dream. Don't worry yourself with such things."

Uriel slowly opened his eyes. Darkness allowed the images of his dreams to continue. His vision adjusted until he was able to make out the face of the one who called him from his sleep.

His grandmother, Mrs. Covington, sat on the edge of his bed. She stroked the side of his face. It tickled. She smiled and kissed him on the cheek. He felt the warm wetness of her lips. She looked younger than she did when he last saw her. Her skin was taunt and tight; her eyes bright and vivid; her hair dark and silky. Mrs. Covington smiled again, then faded into nothingness.

Uriel took a glimpse at the clock. It was 3:33 am. He turned onto his side and went back to sleep assuming that his grandmother was only an extension of a dream.

XI

James sat in his office behind a stack of files, a hot cup of coffee, and a cell phone that seemed to never stop buzzing. *I should have retired years ago!* He thought to himself as he shuffled through piles of invoices. There was no reason for him to be coming into the office. He had a capable staff that could run his car detailing business successfully without him there daily. Now that he and Sadie were on good terms, James truly considered stepping down from his post and passing the reigns to his assistant manager.

His cell phone rang again, this time a picture of Forrest rested upon the screen. James picked up the phone and answered it.

"What up man?" James asked into the phone, a wide smile stretching across his face. "It's been a long time brotha! How you been?"

"Not so good," Forrest unintentionally answered honestly. He planned on small talk and then telling James the bad news, but somehow Forrest thwarted his own plan.

The smile faded from James's face. He stood up from his desk and closed his office door. He put his desk phone on busy and said to his friend, "Talk to me man. What up?"

"It's Sky," Forrest answered; his voice trembling.

"What about Sky?" James asked impatiently. He didn't like the tone of Forrest's voice. James heart began to speed up. "Ya'll not getting' a divorce?"

"No!" Forrest retorted. "A divorce would be better news."

"You scarin' me man. Tell me what's goin' on," James said.

"Sky has cancer," Forrest admitted. "It's bad. She's in stage four. It's in her breasts and lungs." Forrest began to weep.

James was stunned silent. A tear ran down his face.

"Why?" Forrest cried. "We have four children. She's so young. What am I going to do without her?"

"Did ya'll get a second opinion?" James asked, not knowing what to say.

"We got a second and a third. All of the results are the same. I'm a freaking doctor! How the hell did I miss this!" Forrest yelled. "This is my fault. I should have seen it!"

"Man don't do that to yo'self. There is no way you could've known. Doctors can be wrong. God has the final say," James said. "Come to Atlanta. We got some of the best cancer doctors. We got plenty room in the house. You know Sky would feel a heck of a lot betta wit' Sadie by her side."

"I don't know," Forrest answered. "How do I know that the stress from being in Atlanta didn't cause the cancer in the first place?"

Forrest's words were a kick to the groin for James. He felt as if Forrest was blaming Sky's cancer on his family. Last time the Cohen's were in Atlanta, Sky, pregnant with Mars, battled the angel (Khalid's father) who had possessed James's mother-in-law, Mrs. Covington. Sky was a little battered and bruised but not seriously injured. She was able to deliver a healthy baby and leave town safely after the incident. James didn't know how the incident could have caused cancer, but he understood that his friend was searching for answers and James's years of being with Sadie taught him that nothing was too farfetched.

"I don't know," James whispered. "I understand if ya'll don't wanna come, but thangs are different now. Khalid is in college. The angel is gone. I think all that creepy stuff is over. Do whateva you gotta do. I got yo back either way."

"Thanks bro," Forrest answered. "I got to go back to work. I just wanted to tell you what was going on. I'll call Luis later, when I am ready. I just needed to tell someone. Don't tell Sadie before Sky does. She would be really angry with me if she knew that I just told you."

"Okay," James said. "Take it easy."

Forrest hung up the phone.

James put his cell phone in his pocket and picked up his jacket. He walked out of the office and headed straight home. He knew that he needed to be there to catch Sadie when she fell.

XII

"Hey girlie!" Sky greeted through the computer's video chat camera as she sat braiding Venus's hair into a big fishtail.

Venus rolled her eyes. Her mother feigning happiness made her skin itch. Venus felt that all that fake grinning her mother was doing was absolutely ridiculous. How could a dying woman pretend to be so happy?

"Hey!" Sadie responded, waving her hand at Venus and Sky from her kitchen table in Atlanta.

Venus sarcastically smirked and smacked her lips. She crossed her arms and refused to respond to Sadie's greeting.

"Are you finished?" Venus snapped at her mother. "I got something to do!"

"Yes," Sky responded letting the big braid drop and allowing her riled daughter to excuse herself.

"What's going on with her?" Sadie asked surprised that Sky allowed Venus to get away with such ornery behavior. Usually Sky would grab her child up by the arm and reprimand her for using such a disrespectful tone.

"Venus is just acting out," Sky responded. "Don't mind her. She's going through a lot right now. We all are."

"Is everything okay?" Sadie asked before taking a sip of the steaming tea sitting in front of her.

"Not really." Sky answered. She flopped back on the sofa and took a deep breath. "Nothing is okay. I'm not sure if anything will ever be okay again."

Sadie put the tea cup down and asked, "What's going on?"

"I'm sick Sadie," Sky whispered.

"What do you mean?" Sadie asked; her face filling with fear. Sky was never sick. Sadie had known Sky for most of her life and she could not remember her having a cold or even a headache.

"I found a lump in my armpit and in my breast. I had a biopsy and the results revealed that I have stage four cancer," Sky said. She laughed a little and continued, "And I figured the lumps were an allergic reaction to my deodorant."

"Oh, Sky!" Sadie began to cry a loud guttural cry that pushed every bit of air from her lungs. The thought of losing her best friend made Sadie want to scream, cuss, pray, fight, feel nothing ever again. "I'll be there first thing in the morning," she slobbered.

"First of all, you need to get a hold of yourself. All that snot running down your nose ain't cute! Looking at your blubbering makes me feel worse than I already do, so stop it! Second of all, you don't have to do that," Sky said. "I don't need you running up here upsetting my children and husband with your emotional craziness. We got enough going on without you snottin' and cryin'! If they see you carrying on, they'll think I'm dyin' for sure."

"I'm coming!" Sadie cried out like a toddler. "And you can't do anything about it!"

"Shut up all that cryin' girl!" Sky spat through tears involuntarily falling from her eyes. "Now you got me cryin'! I'm not dead yet!"

"Don't say that! You aren't going to die!" Sadie wept; her tears making Sky's image blurrier by the second.

"According to the doctor, I can croak at any minute," Sky croaked like a frog.

"It's not funny Sky," Sadie mewled. "I can't lose you. I've lost Mama and Daddy already. You, James, and the kids are all I have left. You are my rock Sky. What will I do without you?"

"I don't want to lose me either! I hate the thought of not seeing my babies become adults. I hate that my beautiful husband may seek comfort in another woman's arms after I am dead. I hate that I may not live to see forty-five. I hate that you and I can't travel the world like Oprah and Gail. I hate that they are telling me that I am so far along that no amount of chemotherapy or radiation will help. They just want me to take a pain pill and damn die!" Sky screamed; her reddish-brown face curling at every corner.

"I'm sorry Sky. I didn't mean to upset you. Forgive me for being selfish," Sadie whined. "I can't imagine what you and your family are going through."

Sky wiped her tears with her forearms and nodded her head instantly forgiving Sadie.

"Did you get a second opinion?" Sadie asked through sniffs.

"Yes, and a third. I went to the best doctors in the northeast and they all agreed with Dr. Izan," answered Sky.

"Well, you need to get another opinion from the best doctor in the southeast!" yelped Sadie. "You have to come down here, so I can help take care of you. I will come up there to help you and the family pack."

"I don't think that's a good idea," Sky admitted. "Forrest may not want us in your home. He blames my confrontation with the angel for the cancer."

There was no rebuttal that Sadie could give. It was possible that Sky was harmed when the angel struck her so many years ago. There was no telling what preternatural effect that could have had on her body.

"Is Mars okay?" Sadie asked. "You were carrying Mars when you fought the angel inside of my mother. If he is okay, then the cancer could have come from somewhere else."

"Yes, Mars is okay. Forrest had him tested for everything under the son after my diagnosis. His health is perfect," answered Sky.

"If you can't come here, please let me come to you," Sadie begged.

"I will talk to Forrest and the children and see what they think is best. Don't come tomorrow. I promise I will get back to you soon. Okay?" Sky asked leaning towards the computer screen.

"Okay," Sadie reluctantly responded.

"Talk to you later," Sky said and blew her best friend a kiss. "Pray for me!"

Sadie waved goodbye and closed her laptop. She folded her arms and dropped her head over the computer and wept until Uriel walked into the kitchen.

"Mom," Uriel called out. He rushed to her and wrapped his arm around her shoulder. "Are you okay?"

"No, baby. I am not okay," Sadie confessed. "Sit down baby."

Uriel grabbed the chair next to her and did as he was told.

"Auntie Sky is very sick," Sadie wept. "Very sick."

"Don't cry mom," Uriel tried to sooth. "She will be alright."

"You don't understand," Sadie wailed. "She has cancer. Stage four cancer."

"God can do all things," Uriel coaxed. "Have faith."

Sadie looked into his eyes; his pure optimistic eyes. She wished that she could believe how he believed. She smiled and touched his cheek.

He kissed her hand.

"Trust me mom. I will never lie to you. Auntie Sky will be just fine," Uriel assured his mother with a kiss on the forehead before leaving the house for math tutoring.

XIII

"Psi Kappa Nu!" a large group of young men wearing red and blue shirts chanted as they stepped to an intricate rhythm. They danced and twirled canes in the courtyard of the university as students gathered around them to watch the show.

Khalid and Yvette watched from a nearby bench as the men screamed and grunted to a new found beat. Yvette sat on Khalid's knee clapping and cheering every time one of the fraternity members jumped, spun, or did a flip.

"You're really into this huh?" Khalid asked more intrigued by Yvette's excitement than the frat boys. The weight of her body bouncing on his knee made his leg numb.

"Yeah. They fire!" she squealed. "They fine too! You should pledge. You totally look like a Psi Kappa Nu man."

"I don't join crews. Crews join me," Khalid commented. "I'm bored. Let's go back to my room."

"We always in yo' room. Why can't we chill around campus sometime? You shamed of me?" Yvette grumbled.

Khalid pushed her from his knee onto the bench and stood up. "Save the drama for your mama. I've been out here chillin' with you all day. We ate lunch together at the student center, we went to the bookstore, and now I'm sitting in the hot sun, so you can see them lames jump around like idiots. So, you can miss me with all that you talkin' 'bout. I'm finna go."

Khalid started towards his dorm and Yvette followed on his heels, struggling to keep the pace.

"Sorry," she pouted. Desperation peppered her voice. Every day she worried about if she could keep his interest; if he would remain her man. Several different women had been spotted with him around campus. Yvette would catch them alone and threaten to beat them up if they saw him again. This worked for most girls, but there were a few persistent ones that Yvette figured she would have to actually fight.

"You good," Khalid answered as he held open the door to the dorm. They walked down the hall and turned the corner. From the end of the hall, whiffs of lavender smoke floated from the bottom of Khalid's door. Khalid softly pushed Yvette backward and ran towards his room.

Lavender smoke whiffed from the cracks of Khalid's dorm room door like tails of dancing genies. The ascending vapor twirled its way to the ceiling and evaporated. He slowly opened the door.

The room was a cloud of purple; thick with the smell of myrrh. The cloudiness began to thin out and a thin silhouette came into view. In the center of the room, Belial stood within a circle of what appeared to be made of a white powdery substance. Glowing, flickering orbs of light encircled Belial within the circle. At first glance, Khalid thought that they were candles of hanging lights suspended from some unknown source, but upon further observation, he discovered that they were tiny life forces darting sporadically. The lightning bug like creatures emitted a pale white light as Belial whispered something indecipherable. Their buzzing made a music so foreign yet so familiar. Chills of joy and fear cascaded down his spine as the buzzing became louder and louder. It called to him like an ancestral hymn. Khalid began to hum then stopped himself for he felt if he continued, he would be consumed with ecstasy and driven to frenzy as if dancing to the flute of Bacchus. Khalid focused his eyes upon one of the glowing creatures. He gasped. The glowing creature had a human shape.

Belial looked up from his murmurings and smiled. The head of his shadow was still looking down.

"You are home early my friend," he grumbled, and with a wave of his hand, the powdery circle dissolved into the floor. All traces were gone. Belial lifted the lid of the ancient box which sat on his desk, and the light beings flew inside. The top dropped, and their musical buzzing was silenced. Within moments, the fog had cleared, and the dorm looked as if nothing peculiar had ever occurred.

Khalid stood at the threshold; eyes unblinking and speechless. Yvette, seeing his body standing as stiff as a pole, hurried over to his side and peered into the room seeing nothing but Belial standing in the middle of the floor with a mischievous grin on his face.

"What's going on," she asked; grabbing Khalid's forearm and waving her free hand in front of his eyes. "Khalid!" she yelled.

He said nothing; his eyes locked with Belial's and they both stood paralyzed by each other's stare.

Yvette stepped between the two. Khalid looked at Yvette and breathed for the first time in what seemed like an eternity.

"What's going on?" Yvette asked; her small hands holding the sides of his face. "Are you okay?"

"Of course, he is okay," Belial interjected. "He's just overwhelmed by the call of his people."

"What the hell you talkin' 'bout weirdo," Yvette snapped with her hand on her hips. "You must have been smokin' some kinda grape weed or somethin'."

Belial looked at her like a cockroach that needed to be squashed. He turned to Khalid and said, "When you are ready to find out what you are truly capable of, let me know and we can explore what's in my box."

Khalid nodded.

"I'll give you two some privacy," Belial said as he walked towards the door. His shadow lingered for a moment then joined its master.

Yvette clung to Khalid, thinking that she had imagined the shadow's delayed movement.

Belial left the room and the door slammed behind him without anyone touching it.

"That's one weird S.O.B.." Yvette whispered as Khalid pulled her to the bed and allowed all the frenzy he felt within him to be unleashed into her.

X|V

Fridays were always frantic at school for the Cohen kids. All four of them attended Madaraka Academy; a top-notch private school in the center of Manhattan where they were absorbed in culture and received the best education the city had to offer. For the most part, they enjoyed their studies and looked forward to each day. All except for Earth, who was occasionally bullied, but not too badly because her big sister Venus was never too far away; for Venus was vicious and when she sought revenge, it was swift and unmerciful. So much so that Earth was weary of telling her sister when someone was bothering her, but sometimes the wrath of Venus was needed to make the harassment stop.

Earth walked down the hallway trying not to bump into the constant flow of rushing children. Noise filled the halls as they laughed, fought, and slammed locker doors. Earth moseyed along in her plaid skirt, white button-down shirt, and knee-high socks. A green book bag with a picture of a brown girl with a huge afro was swung over her shoulder. Her red hair was pulled into two giant pony tails and cherry flavored lip-gloss made her lips glisten. A big bubble gum bubble came from her mouth and popped before she started to chew the pink wad again.

"Earth!" a voice called from a classroom behind her. "Earth!"

Earth turned around and allowed her eyes to search the hall until they stopped on a short alabaster girl with long blonde hair. The girl was plump and pretty with chubby cheeks and eyes that were as blue as the sky. She wore her uniform a size too big which made her look a size bigger than she was. Braces with pink rubber bands covered her large teeth. She waved her hand wildly until Earth started towards her.

"Hey Simone! What's up?" Earth asked; one arm holding books and the other resting on her narrow hip.

"Can I come over your house after school to finish our project," Simone asked. An overabundance of saliva accented every word making the grossest sound Earth had ever heard.

"Swallow!" Earth snapped. She had to tell Simone that often. She was known around the school as Slobbery Simone.

Simone swallowed.

"Sorry. I'm not used to these braces and I just finished eating candy. My mouth is so juicy," Simone admitted with a loud slurp.

Earth shook her head and laughed at her friend. Simone was sweet, but the epitome of a dork. Everything about her was awkward from her snorting laugh to her clumsiness. Yet, she was extremely comfortable in her skin. Earth loved that about her. Simone's self-confidence was astounding. She was the type of girl who would fearlessly walk up to the captain of the football team and ask him to prom, and if he declined, Simone would waste no time heading to the next beautiful boy who caught her eye.

"I will ask my mom and will let you know later on," Earth said. The bell rang. "I gotta go to class. See you after school!"

"Okay, bye!" Simone slurped as she headed in the opposite direction.

Earth turned and bolted down the hall until she reached the door of the chemistry lab. She opened the door, but it slammed in her face subsequently hitting her right knee. Earth opened the door again and limped into the classroom. A bright red bruise began to form on her knee.

The students laughed. The teacher was absent, probably on a bathroom break.

"Ouch!" Earth screamed. "Why did you do that?" she asked a tall brown girl with an evil grin on her face. The girl had long, straight, black hair that hung to the top of her thighs. Deceptively, her face looked pleasant.

"Because I wanted to," Ishanvi said as she stood with her arms crossed waiting for Earth to pass her by, so she could trip her. Ishanvi stuck her foot out and Earth stumbled. Ishanvi and the class laughed as Earth moaned in pain.

"You better leave her alone before her sister beats you to sleep," a boy sitting in the back of the classroom said between laughs.

"Whatever Andre'!" Ishanvi snapped. "I'll slap the crap out of her and her sister."

The class gasped. It was clear that Ishanvi did not know who Earth's sister was because if she did, she would not have spoken so recklessly.

"I bet you won't," Andre' dared.

"Why are you always instigating?" Earth asked. "I'm okay. There is no need to bring my sister into this. Just let it go. Why do you want to see a fight?"

"Because I don't like that grimy girl! I don't know how people act in India, but I want to see your sister put Ishanvi in her place!" Andre' answered, his big lips twisting to one side. His dark skin was beautiful and smooth, the color of onyx. His hair was braided neatly into four cornrows on the top and faded on the sides.

Earth found him extremely attractive, but also extremely annoying. She hated that his primary job at school was not to learn, but to instigate. Andre' was the source of more than half the fights in tenth grade. Maybe he wanted to be a boxing promoter when he grew up.

"I'm not from India. My parents are! I'm an American from New York City. Who you calling grimy?" Ishanvi screamed, her eyes cutting in every direction.

"You!" Andre' answered. "A matter of fact, I am going to call your bluff!" He picked up his cell phone and sent a text to Venus saying that her sister Earth was being bullied and the bully was also threatening to beat her up as well. He said that the bully wanted to meet after school off campus outside of the local pizza joint. Venus, being the brawler that she was, quickly agreed.

"Ishanvi, Venus will meet you after school in front of Michael Angelo's Pizza," the boy confirmed. "I'm taking bets. I got my money on Venus. Who you got?" he asked the class as he pulled a twenty-dollar bill out of his pocket and slammed it on the desk.

Upon hearing Venus's name, Ishanvi felt like she had signed her death certificate. She had no idea that Venus was Earth's sister. They looked nothing alike. Visually, there was no way Ishanvi could have known. One was brown. The other was pale and red. One was thin. The other was curvy. Earth was faint hearted and passive. Venus was like Muhammad Ali. She hit hard and knew how to bob and weave. She fought like a boy but looked like a glamor girl. No one had ever landed a punch on her beautiful face. Ishanvi was terrified, but she knew there was no avoiding Venus. If Ishanvi didn't show up, Venus would come looking for her and the beating would most likely be worse.

The class pulled out cash and placed their bets on Venus as well. Andre' collected the money in his backpack and passed out receipts for bets.

Earth sat in the back of the classroom with tears in her eyes. As much as she disliked Ishanvi, she hated to see Venus fight because there was something cruel and unnerving about the joy Venus found in violence, and since the news of their mother's cancer, the violent, murky hole in Venus's heart had only grown larger.

XV

"How are you feeling?" Forrest asked, tucking a wild tangled curl behind Sky's ear.

"I don't know," she answered before taking a sip of tea.

They sat in the middle of their favorite Manhattan café. People on laptops filled most tables and the others were filled with elderly people reading newspapers. The sound of traffic thundering outside competed with the slow jazz playing from the café speakers. A bubbly waitress sat two muffins in front of the couple and disappeared through the kitchen door.

"Did you think about the treatment that Dr. Izan suggested?" Forrest asked.

Whipped cream from the hot cocoa he sipped gave him a fluffy mustache. In one swipe, Sky removed the cream and sucked it off her finger.

"Thank you," Forrest added.

"You're welcome," said Sky, looking over the crowd of elderly people. An overwhelming since of jealousy filled her. She would never whine about her ginger hair transitioning to silver. She would never get a chance to lament over wrinkles. She would never get a chance to complain to Sadie about arthritis or incontinence. Sky would never get a chance to decide which child she would live with when she was too old to live alone. She would never see her grandchildren. She would never get to be a mother-in-law that her children's spouses would simply adore. She would never get to see the world with Forrest. She may never get to see tomorrow. Sky began to cry.

"Honey," Forrest called. He picked up a napkin from the table and began to wipe her eyes. "Everything will be alright."

"No, it won't!" she yelled louder than she intended. "I want to move to Atlanta. I want to have my family and my best friend near me."

"Sadie can come here," Forrest suggested.

The thought of moving to Atlanta troubled him to an extent he was not aware of. The mention of the city caused a burning sensation in the pit of his stomach.

"I can get another opinion in Atlanta. It's warmer there. I want to be able to enjoy my last days," Sky confessed, her red rimmed eyes wild with desperation.

"I don't think Atlanta is safe. Do you remember what happened the last time we were there?" Forrest asked between his teeth.

"They haven't been troubled by that thing since Uriel casted it out," Sky replied. She took a sip of tea and tried to calm herself. People had begun watching.

"Sadie's house is safe. Besides, Khalid is gone to college and we can buy our own place. Transitioning to a hospital in Atlanta will be easy for you. With your reputation, the city would love to have you back," she said.

"I don't feel comfortable with moving our family to Atlanta," Forrest retorted. "There is nothing for us there that we don't have here. The school year just started. Do you want to pull our children away from their friends? They may lose credits"

"They also have friends in Atlanta. They are very close to Sadie's children. Besides, all our children are way above grade level. They can transfer and not lose anything. Sadie gave me a list of excellent private and public schools in Atlanta," Sky said.

"Our kids are not going to public school," Forrest huffed. "That's out of the question."

"Imma product of public school! I turned out okay," Sky laughed.

"You also say Imma, so I consider you lucky," Forrest retorted and sipped on his cocoa.

Sky continued, "Seriously, I want to move to Atlanta."

"I don't," Forrest responded. "There is enough for me to worry about with your health. I don't want any added pressure with Sadie and her son."

"I don't want to argue." She took a deep breath. "I am the one dying."

"That's not fair," Forrest spat. "I can't believe you would go so low!"

"What choice did you leave me?" Sky laughed.

Tears came, and she laughed hard and loud. She cried and laughed until her voice was hoarse. She understood his perspective, but she needed her family and her friend.

Forrest's frown softened, and he smiled. He reached across the table and placed his hand on hers.

"I'm sorry," Sky whimpered. "I want everyone I love near me. I know that moving to Atlanta is hard for you. I understand your concerns and your fears. I brought up the idea to the children and they seem open. There is nothing keeping us in New York. Your parents moved to Florida years ago. You can work in Atlanta. As a writer, I can work anywhere. Aren't you tired of the cold and the noise and the pollution and the rude cab drivers and the expensive cost of living? Just think about it. Okay?"

"Okay," he answered. The burning in his stomach magnified as he forced a smile. "Let's go home."

Forrest stood up and pulled Sky's chair out. She reached inside of her purse and pulled out her wallet.

"I already paid the waitress," Forrest said.

"I know," Sky responded as she dropped a crisp one-hundred-dollar bill on the table and followed her husband out of the door.

"That was a big tip for two beverages," Forrest commented; warmed by his wife's generosity.

"When you're blessed, bless," she replied locking arms with Forrest and leaning her head on his shoulder as they exited the building to begin their stroll down the streets of New York City.

XVI

The school bell rang, and the students poured out into the streets of Manhattan. A small group congregated outside of Michael Angelo's Pizza shop waiting for Venus and Ishanvi to show up. Andre' ran inside of the pizza shop to give Angelo fifty dollars so he would not call the police. The immoral old man gladly took the money and handed Andre' back five dollars to place a bet on Venus. Andre' took the money and handed the greasy pizza shop owner a receipt. He exited the shop and stood on top of an iron chair and began to stir the crowd into a blood thirsty frenzy.

Venus came with Earth and Camille pulling on her arm and begging her to go home. Venus shook her sister and her friend off and waited for Ishanvi to show her face.

"I'm going home!" Camille declared. "I can't watch this." She turned and walked away. Violence was not her thing. Camille had seen Venus in action before and the results were never pretty.

"You don't have to do this!" Earth begged. "She's not worth it Vee. Mom would be so mad if you get into trouble again."

"She'll be even madder if I allowed you to be bullied!" Venus belted and snatched her arm away. "If you touch me again, I'm going to beat you up too!'

Ishanvi and her crew slowly turned the corner. The crowd went wild.

Venus pulled her long black hair into a ponytail and pinned up the loose hair, then pulled a small jar of petroleum jelly out of her purse and rubbed it all over her face to ensure that she would not get many bruises or scratches. Venus took off her school blazer and handed it, her backpack, and purse to Earth.

Ishanvi handed her belongings to her friends and stood in front of Venus. She said, "I don't have a problem with you. Andre' sent you that text. He's trying to make a quick dollar. I didn't say any of that stuff."

"Did you hit my sister with a door and trip her up?" Venus snarled. She shuffled from foot to foot readying herself for battle.

"I was just playing," Ishanvi replied; her voice trembling like a vibrating cell phone. "I don't want to fight you."

"Well, you should have thought about that before you put your hands on my sister!" Venus yelled.

She ran up on Ishanvi and punched her in the face, then stepped back and kicked her in the shin.

The crowd cooed and laughed as Ishanvi rocked from the punch. Grabbing her face and stumbling backward, she never recalled being hit that hard in her life.

Ishanvi swung at Venus wildly, missing Venus with every swing. Venus backhand slapped Ishanvi causing her to stumble backward and Venus followed her throwing blow after blow to the staggering girl's head. Venus gave Ishanvi's head a break and began to plummet her stomach with punches. Vomit poured from Ishanvi's mouth onto Venus's shoes like a sour waterfall. The repugnant liquid angered Venus even more.

"You messed up my favorite shoes!" Venus growled. She started hammering Ishanvi's face again. Skin broke under Venus's punches and blood freckled her swelling knuckles.

The crowd's laughter quickly morphed from glee to grim. They gasped as Ishanvi was beaten brutally. Blood spurted from Ishanvi's mouth. A dark ring formed around her eyes. Venus punched and punched until Ishanvi's face turned to a blackberry. It was nearly unrecognizable.

Earth tried to pull Venus off, but Venus pushed her sister so hard that she hit the ground.

Andre' grabbed Venus in a bear hug and lifted her off the ground. Venus kicked and screamed until the boy was forced to drop her.

"Yo! Chill!" Andre' yelled.

Venus ran back toward the black and blue girl. Andre' pulled Venus backward and told Ishanvi's friends to get her home.

"What's wrong with you?" Andre' asked Venus. "Why did you do her like that? We wanted to see a fight not a massacre!"

Venus looked into his eyes and spit on the ground. She said, "You instigated this whole thing and got what you were looking for, so you should ask yourself what's wrong with you!"

Venus snatched up her belongings and pulled Earth from the ground.

"Let's go!" Venus yelled as she trotted down the street pulling her sister behind her.

XVII

Living in Khalid's dorm room was a hard task. Every time Khalid looked around, Belial had his eyes on him. When Khalid studied, Belial sat on his bed and watched Khalid unabashedly. The pale young man sat in a hypnotic state studying Khalid's every move. Rarely Belial spoke; he just watched and smiled a smile so sinister that Khalid would leave the room. For a week Khalid had been enduring Belial's stares. It was time for them to stop.

"What is your problem?" Khalid hissed and slammed his book closed. "Why every time I look up, you're looking at me?"

Belial grinned.

Khalid stood up from his bed and towered over Belial who was sitting at his desk.

"Answer me when I talk to you!" Khalid demanded; his fist in balls and his eyes wild.

"Or what?" Belial questioned; the grin on his face even bigger. The lamplight caused a shadow to fall across his face that changed his features to something nonhuman. Khalid stepped backward.

"Just stop looking at me. I can't concentrate!" Khalid huffed. He sat back on his bed full of vexation.

"I apologize," Belial cackled. "You just remind me so much of your father."

Khalid swallowed hard. Tension formed in the pit of his belly. He had not seen or heard from his father in nearly a decade. Last time he had heard from Turiel, he was speaking through the mouth of Khalid's grandmother, Mrs.

Covington, whom the fallen angel had possessed. Uriel's exorcism of Turiel caused her death.

"You know my father?" Khalid asked, almost too weak to push the words out.

"Know him is a stretch." Belial said. "I know of him, and I know how to contact him."

"How?" Khalid asked.

"I'll let you know when you are ready to explore what's in my box," Belial said and stood up. "I know you are curious." His eerie eyes danced in the lamplight giving him an otherworldly appearance that stabbed at every instinct that Khalid had to run. Only his pride and curiosity kept him seated.

It was true. Ever since Khalid saw those flying lights, he could not get them off his mind. He spent days researching ghosts, fairies, energy orbs, anything that may have explained what they were. He talked to Yvette about it and instantly regretted it because it opened the door for her to tell him about all the ghost sightings her family had witnessed. Khalid had no interest in the tales of spooked out root workers and their inebriated cohorts.

Belial made his way to the door, his shadow still standing by the desk.

"I have class," Belial said. "See you in a bit." Belial disappeared from the room; his shadow stayed put.

The black shade moved an inch and Khalid grabbed his keys and cell phone and bolted from the room. He ran down the hall past Belial and out of the building. He could hear Belial laughing down the hall. Thoughts of Uriel filled

Khalid's mind. As he walked across the yard, he pulled his phone from his pocket and called his brother.

"Hey!" Uriel answered with excitement in his voice. He was always happy to hear from Khalid.

"Hey," Khalid responded, his voice higher than normal.

"What's the matter?" Uriel asked. He was at school, but at lunch so he could talk for a moment. "You sound weird."

"I think I'm going crazy," Khalid admitted. "My roommate; there is something really off about him." Khalid sat down under a tree where few students lingered.

"Why you say that?" Uriel asked. He stood up from his lunch table and threw his tray in the trash. He asked for permission to go outside, and then found himself a tree to sit under.

"It's his shadow. It moves without him," Khalid said. The words sounded crazy coming out of his mouth. He felt stupid for saying them.

"What do you mean?" Uriel asked.

"Just what I said," Khalid snapped. "The dude will walk away, and his shadow will still be in the same spot or he will move, and the shadow will make a contrary movement."

"That's scary," Uriel said for lack of better words. "Pray about it."

"There you go," Khalid sighed. "Prayer has never helped a single person in human history."

"It helps me all the time," Uriel said. "I prayed for Mom and Dad and they are happy again. I prayed that angel wouldn't come back, and he never did. I prayed that grandma's soul was okay after she died, and I think I saw her in a dream or something the other night, and she looked happy. God answers pr..."

"Whatever," Khalid hissed cutting Uriel off. Uriel talking about prayer and God made Khalid more unnerved than Belial did.

"Why did you call me if you didn't want my help?" Uriel asked; a little hurt by his brother's disregard. "You're the one living with a Scooby-Doo character, not me!"

Khalid laughed.

"I didn't mean to be like that. Calm down," Khalid laughed. "Sorry."

"It's okay," Uriel forgave.

"And another thing, he has this box. It looks older than anything I have ever seen. It looks like it belongs in a museum or something. There are strange symbols all over it, and last week I caught him performing some sort of ritual and these things that look like lightening bugs were flying all around him. Music came from their movement. When I came close to one, it looked like a small person or something. I didn't see wings or anything. They were just flying around like a bunch of Peter Pans. When Belial saw me walk in, he waved them away and they went into the box. Tell me I'm not losing it." Khalid said. He leaned against the tree trunk and waited.

"I know you don't trust my process but let me pray on it and I will get back to you," Uriel said. "God always answers my prayers."

As much as he hated to admit it, Khalid knew that Uriel had some kind of special intuition which made him privy to things no one could understand. Whether it was God or an incredible sense of discernment, Khalid knew that it worked.

"Khalid be careful. Remember the dream I had about you wrestling a shadow? Maybe it was warning you about your roommate," Uriel advised. "I got to go. Lunchtime is over. Talk to you later."

Khalid disconnected the call and put his cellphone back into his pocket. He had forgotten about Uriel's dream. Khalid wondered what it all meant.

XVIII

"How you holdin' up?" James whispered into Sadie's ear as they cuddled in bed. He pulled her close to him so that they would be a perfect spoon; folded into one another like a continuous being. The warmth of their nude bodies fought against the room made cool by the ceiling fan swirling around. In the darkness, they laid silently until Sadie decided to answer her husband's question.

"I don't know," she admitted. "Sky has been my best friend my whole life. I don't know what to do if I lose her. I'm still not over Mama and Daddy dying."

"I talked to Forrest again today. He comin' to visit next week to see a few places," James said before kissing his wife's neck.

Sadie's head popped up.

"Are they coming down here?" Sadie asked.

"Naw. Just Forrest," James answered.

"Sky said that Forrest was against them moving to Atlanta, and she won't even let me come up to visit her," said Sadie. "Why would she want to battle cancer alone? I just want to be there for her like she was for me when I needed her."

"She ain't alone. Sky has a husband and children," James said. "You gotta respect what she and Forrest decide," James advised. "I know ya'll tight like jeans too small, but this is a fragile time for her and her family. Don't be selfish Sadie. It ain't about how you feel right now."

"I know," Sadie groaned. "I just want to see her. That's all."

"You will," James replied.

"How do you know?" Sadie asked.

"Well, Forrest called me today and said that Sky is very adamant 'bout moving to Atlanta. She wants our families to be near each other. Forrest ain't happy about it, but he say he owes it to her to come down and consider their options. We 'posed to meet up with Luis. He doesn't know 'bout Sky yet. Forrest say he'll tell him when he gets to Atlanta," James said.

Sadie's face brightened up.

He knew the news would bring a smile to her face. She had been so worried that she may not get to see Sky before it was too late. That would devastate Sadie and James did not want that. He didn't want anything that could ruin their bliss. If he had things his way, he would leave everyone behind and relocate somewhere far away, but he knew that would never happen. James hadn't had things his way in eons, so he settled for things being as good as they could be at the moment.

"I hope they decide to come. It would be nice to have Sky near," Sadie admitted. "The children would love to see her children. I know they miss each other. Uriel and Earth and Khalid and Venus talk on the phone all the time. It would be nice for them to be able to see each other more often."

"I feel ya. I kinda miss Forrest too. I ain't got nobody to beat in basketball and I'm tired of beating Uriel and Luis," James laughed. "The trio gone be back in effect!"

"Oh Lord. You three knuckleheads are too much!" Sadie laughed. "It will be like the good old days before everything went awry." Sadie's laugh faded. Sadness filled her eyes.

"Leave the past in the past. Things good now. Let it stay that way. Ain't no sense cryin' over spilled milk. None of what happened to our family was yo' fault. I know that, and you know that," James said. He turned her to face him. "The worst is behind us."

Sadie kissed his lips and buried her head in his chest. How she hoped that was true.

"You hear me?" James asked with his nose buried in her metallic silver hair.

"Yes, baby," she whispered. "I hear you."

"Stay happy. We deserve to be happy," James stated as he silently prayed that they would remain that way.

X|X

"Venus why is there blood all over you!" Sky squealed as Venus and Earth walked through the front door of their home.

Venus's white shirt looked like she had fallen in a ripe strawberry patch. Outside of the red splashes and her disheveled clothes, every hair on her head was in place.

Sky rushed over to her eldest daughter and checked her for injuries. She found not even a scratch.

"Venus was fighting again," Earth mumbled under her breath and tried to whisk past her mother to no avail. Sky pulled her by the arm and swung her next to Venus.

"Don't make me knock the freckles off you! What happened and where ya'll been? Jupiter was looking for you for an hour. Mars was crying because he thought both of ya'll were kidnapped! Where the hell have ya'll been?" Sky yelled, her reddish-brown face turning more red than brown. Bracelets clanked every time she moved her hands from her hips to pointing at her daughters.

"Outside of Michael Angelo's Pizza," Earth confessed. "It's a few blocks from the school."

Venus stood with her arms crossed and lips twisted to the side. She rolled her eyes upwards and sighed periodically.

"You better get rid of your attitude before I choke you to sleep!" Sky threatened knowing good and well that her threats were empty; nevertheless, she constantly made them.

Venus rolled her eyes again and said nothing. Half of her felt guilty about making her sick mother worry, but the other half of her was tired of being treated like a child. She was three years from being a legal adult and she felt her mother was still treating her like she was three.

Jupiter and Mars came into the living room to watch the commotion. Seeing Sky and Venus interact was always more entertaining than watching social media videos. They sat on the sofa bursting with anticipation. The boys laughed under their breath. Venus was always in trouble for something or another.

"What were you doing all the way over there, Venus?" Sky asked; her face so close to Venus's that they could do an Eskimo kiss.

Venus said nothing. She let out a huge sigh through her nose.

Sky grabbed Venus's arm and spat, "You better answer when I ask you a question!"

Venus shook her arm free. Rage contorted her pretty brown face. Hot tears ran down her cheeks.

"I was defending Earth! Some girl had hit her with a door and tripped her up," Venus growled.

Sky turned to Earth and asked, "Is this true?"

"Yes, but I told Venus not to fight her," Earth whined. "I begged her not to go to the pizza shop. I hate to see Venus fight! She almost beat that girl to death!"

Earth could never understand why Venus was so protective of her. When they were home, Venus barely spoke to her and when she did, they were not kind words.

"Venus, I understand that you were trying to defend your sister, but you have got to stop fighting. What if that little girl's parents press charges? What are you going to do then?" Sky asked. She couldn't be truly angry because she raised her children to defend and protect each other at all costs. She had no idea that Venus would take things to the extreme. Sky's other children hardly ever was in conflict with anyone. Venus, however, was a natural hell raiser.

"I don't know," Venus sulked. "Can I go to my room now?"

"Go clean yourself up," Sky instructed, a bit of worry contorting her brow. "Earth go do your homework."

Earth went into her room and Venus into hers.

Venus's room was decorated to perfection. A full-sized canopy bed sat in the middle of the room with royal purple sheers hanging from it. Miscellaneous artwork decorated her walls providing splashes of bright color complementing her purple bedspread and curtains. A vanity filled with lip-glosses, earrings, and hair accessories sat next to her bed. A dresser, floor mirror, two turquoise velvet chairs, a floral area rug, and a computer desk completed her room.

Venus walked inside of her walk-in closet where her clothes were organized by color. She was a bit of a neatnik. Everything had its place and she could tell if anything had been tampered with.

In one swift movement, she removed her bloody shirt and tossed it into her bathroom sink to run cold water over it. She did not want the blood stains to stick. It was her favorite white shirt. For a moment, Venus thought about beating Ishanvi up again for messing up her shirt, and she would wear one of Earth's shirts while doing it. Venus laughed at the thought.

Venus jumped into the shower and let the hot water run over her. Her knuckles stung. She looked down and noticed that they were swollen and red like cherry tomatoes. She washed and toweled dry then returned to her bedroom where she changed into a cotton dress and picked up her cell phone.

Anger continued to fill her insides, bubbling up like the foam floating on water when boiling pasta. Venus couldn't decide who made her angrier; her mother or the girl who hit her sister. Both got on her last nerve. It was impossible for her to ever take it out on Sky, so the girl was a great outlet for Venus's anger. Now that the fight was over, her anger still boiled, and she needed to talk to someone who could get her mind off her troubles. She decided to call Khalid. Hearing his voice always made things better. He understood her. They were twin flames that burned from a split wick.

"Hey stranger!" Khalid said through the phone. "I haven't heard from you in forever."

"Hey!" Venus smiled. Her anger lessoned. She could feel her heartbeat slow. "Whatcha doin'?"

"Chillin' in the student center. Trying to stay away from my weirdo roommate. How about you?" Khalid asked. His voice wavered. Every time he talked to Venus it felt like an electric current shot through him.

"I'm in my room trying to get away from my crazy mama. She's mad because I got into a fight today," Venus explained. "I just wanted someone to talk to."

"Are you okay?" Khalid asked; anger swelling in his voice.

"Hell yeah I'm okay. I beat that girl down!" Venus laughed.

Calm filled Khalid. He began to laugh too.

"What happened?" he asked. He put his foot up on the table in front of him and settled back comfortably on the couch. He was grateful that the room was almost empty.

"This girl named Ishanvi tried to bully Earth, so I bullied her. I beat her until her face looked like chewed up bubble gum," Venus bragged. She looked down at her aching knuckles and smiled.

"I think I love you," Khalid chuckled. "You are definitely the most vicious girl I know."

"Thank you," she cackled. "You like college?"

"Yeah, it's cool. Classes are easy. Girls are easier. Can't get no better than that," Khalid answered.

"Sounds like fun," she said with a hint of jealousy. "You hear about my mom?"

"Yeah, Uriel told me that she was sick, or something then went on a tangent about how she will be healed. I figured she had the flu and Uriel was praying that God would send her some cough medicine."

He waited for a laugh that never came.

"What's going on?" Khalid asked.

"I'm surprised he didn't tell you more since Earth has been on the phone with him crying about it almost every night. She's been carrying on ever since we found out that mom has stage four cancer. She is going to die," Venus answered.

Her face felt hot and she felt like throwing up. Tears pooled in the corners of her eyes and suddenly, she felt the desire to fight. She picked up a stuffed animal from her pillow and ripped one of its eyes off, then tossed it upon the pile of one-eyed animals in the corner of her room.

"I'm so sorry to hear that. If I would have known, I would have called you," Khalid apologized. "Are you okay?"

Venus answered, "I don't know how I feel. I'm kinda numb inside. My mom gets on my nerves, but I love her more than the whole world. I try not to think too much. Things can get really dark inside my head. I…"

He looked up and saw a girl looking at him and listening to his conversation. The nosey girl stared at him shamelessly. When their eyes met, she moved from her table to the one next to the couch he was sitting on.

"Hold on," Khalid told Venus.

Venus agreed; a little hurt that he would put her on hold after such a disconcerting announcement. Venus didn't intend to bloviate about the situation, but she did want to express some of her frustrations.

"May I help you?" he asked the girl whose eyes were glued to him. Her pimpled face couldn't hide her attractive bone structure.

Khalid had the ability to see something beautiful in every woman. The young woman had deep set eyes and was very dark skinned. He guessed that she was North

African or Middle Eastern. Her hair was cut close to her head like a curly helmet. Her eyes reminded him of his father's. They had a glistening quality to them that seemed otherworldly. Her arms were so muscular that it leaned towards masculine. Her clothes were a rainbow of muted grays; layers upon layers of cloth that covered her from head to toe, save for her arms and one leg that seemed to escape the river of cloth when she moved.

"I'm sorry to interrupt," the girl said. "I'm in one of your classes. I knew you were the one I was sent here for after you crippled the professor."

She stood up and walked over to Khalid and held out her hand. He shook it.

"I don't know what you're talking about," he lied.

"My name is Hafeeza. I was sent here to protect you by my coven mother," she said. "She had been seeing visions of you since you were born. You are our dark Lord"

"I don't believe in all that," Khalid huffed and moved away from her. Insanity unnerved him.

"I saw your eyes. You willed the professor's body to fold like paper," she retorted. "I know who you are."

Before he could react, she reached up and ran her fingers through his hair until they landed on the raised birthmark on his scalp --a trinity of sixes.

Khalid knocked her hand away and stood up from the sofa and rushed out of the student center without looking back.

"Khalid!" Venus yelled through the phone. "What happened?"

The strange woman made him forget that he was talking to his friend.

"Some weird ass chick was all in my face talking and acting crazy!" he growled.

"What did she do?" Venus asked.

"She put her fingers in my hair like she knows me or something!" Khalid's heartbeat was off the charts. He walked into his dorm and headed towards his room. "She disrupted my peace!" he spat. "Now I have to go in this room and deal with my freak of a roommate."

"I'll call you back!" Venus hung up the phone before he could say another word. She had problems of her own and was not in the mood to care about anyone else's.

XX

Uriel waited outside of the school for his father to pick him up from basketball practice. James was hardly ever late, but today he was so late that Uriel sat outside on a bench alone. All of his teammates left about twenty minutes earlier. The coaches waited impatiently in their cars for him to leave. Uriel dialed his father's number again for the sixth time. James still wasn't picking up.

Uriel called Sadie and she answered.

"Mom," he called. "Where's dad?"

"He should be there in about three minutes. He left his phone at home. He called me before he left work, and I forgot to tell you that he was running late. I was supposed to call you, but I got distracted. I'm so sorry, baby," Sadie apologized, damning herself for not contacting her son earlier. Her day was so hectic. Between organizing an event for the nuns that she worked for and worrying about Sky, Sadie's mind had been a field of clutter.

"Okay mom." Uriel said. "Talk to you later."

"Sorry baby," Sadie apologized again before she hung up the phone.

Uriel played a game on his phone for about five minutes before James pulled into the school parking lot.

Before his car could stop, the basketball coaches sped off. Uriel opened the car door and asked his father to pop the trunk. Uriel threw his bag into the trunk and got into the car.

"Sorry I'm late, son. I had an appointment at the job that ran over," James said. "You hungry?"

Uriel nodded. He was hungry and tired. He leaned back in his seat and put his feet up on the dashboard. He let his eyes close for a moment. The scent of rosewater filled his nose. He opened his eyes. His grandmother, Mrs. Covington was sitting in the back seat of the car directly behind James. She rested her hand on the top of Uriel's head. Her fingers toyed with his thick hair.

"What do you want?" Uriel whispered.

Mrs. Covington looked at him and smiled. She ran the back of her hand across his cheek. Her hand was warm and soft and smelled like rosewater.

"I want you to take care of your brother," she said. She allowed her hand to linger upon his cheek.

"Okay," Uriel agreed.

"Uriel," James called. "Get up!"

Uriel let his seat up.

"You were talkin' in yo' sleep. You sounded like two different people. You creeped me out!" James exclaimed. He had very little tolerance for anything out of the ordinary.

Uriel hesitated for a moment trying to decide if he was going to share his experience with his father. James didn't like to hear anything of a supernatural nature. When anyone brought up anything bizarre, he exited the conversation. Something inside nagged Uriel to share. It felt important, like Khalid's life depended on it.

"I had a dream about grandma. It seemed so real. She was telling me to take care of Khalid," Uriel said. He was sure that he had not slept long enough to enter REM. Something about the encounter felt too real to be a dream. The scent of rosewater was still in the air.

"It was just a dream," James reiterated. He had experienced enough ghosts and goblins in his lifetime. There was no room for more.

Within minutes, James pulled into the parking lot of a barbeque joint. They exited the car and entered the establishment. Black and white pictures of famous people lined the walls. Checkered table cloths were on each table, and the blues rumbled from the speakers.

They sat down and ordered their meals.

Uriel sat quietly; his brows furrowed.

"What's wrong?" James asked hesitantly.

"Khalid called me the other day about his roommate. There is something crazy going on with him," Uriel answered. "He sounded kinda scared. Dad, you know Khalid ain't scared of nobody!"

"What he say?" James asked.

Sweat started to form on his brow. He knew something he didn't want to hear was coming.

"He said that his roommate's shadow was moving differently than the roommate, and that the dude had some kind of old box with fairies or something in it," Uriel answered. He realized how ridiculous the words sounded leaving his mouth. If not for his family history, he would not believe them himself.

A morbidly obese old man wearing an apron stained with years of barbeque sauce sat a platter full of ribs in front of James and Uriel. He wore a gap-toothed smile and a fuzzy afro. People around the neighborhood called him Pops.

Pops placed, beside the ribs, a big bowl of potato salad, a bowl of baked beans, and a bowl of dinner rolls. The fat man waited for them to take a bite and hum their pleasure. It was customary for him to do so. Pops needed to see the joy his food brought. James and Uriel hummed after the first delicious bite and nodded their heads as they went in for a second bite. Pops gave them a thumbs-up and told them that the waitress would be back with their sweet teas before he wobbled back into the kitchen.

"I don't wanna talk about this," James said between bites.

"What if Khalid's in trouble?" Uriel asked holding a rib in front of his mouth, but too fretful to bite it.

"Lid can take care of hisself!" James thundered under his breath. "Don't worry yo' mama with this nonsense and you stay away from that campus!"

Uriel dropped the rib on the plate and fell against the back of his chair. His appetite was gone.

"You hear me boy?" James asked; barbeque sauce all over his mouth.

Uriel said nothing.

"I ain't playin' wit' you!" James said through his teeth; meat stuck between a few of them.

Uriel nodded. Guilt pulled at him for he knew that he could never not help his brother. Disobedience to his father was imminent.

XXI

After the brutal beating Venus had given her, Ishanvi went home to two horrified parents. They instantly called the police, but Ishanvi would not provide any information about her abuser and she begged her parents to drop the case. They took her to the hospital but refused to let her stay home from school after she was discharged. Ishanvi was forced to walk the halls full of shame and embarrassment as punishment for not telling her parents who beat her up. The Patel family finally pried the information from one of their daughter's friends and extended an invitation to the Cohen's to come to their home to talk about the incident. The Cohen's accepted cautiously.

Forrest, Sky, Venus, and Earth arrived at the Patel home at 7 o'clock sharp. Jupiter volunteered to babysit Mars and they both promised to pray for Venus not to go to jail. Neither of them thought Venus would be happy in an orange jumpsuit. Orange was her least favorite color.

Forrest nervously asked the doorman of the Patel's Upper East Side apartment building to buzz them up. The family filed into the elevator and watched the flashing numbers as they climbed to the 13th floor.

"This can't be good," Sky said under her breath.

It was rare to see a building with a thirteenth floor. Many builders considered the number thirteen bad luck. Sky half expected the Patels to answer the door with machetes in their hands.

The Cohens waked down the hall and tapped on door thirteen.

"You got to be kidding me," Sky huffed. "Apartment thirteen on the thirteenth floor? We just entered the Twilight Zone!"

Forrest knocked on the door three times and waited. A short, balding Indian man with medium brown skin and matching brown polyester pants opened the door.

"Mr. Patel?" Forrest asked.

"Yes," the man answered with a thick Indian accent and a slight lisp so his *yes* sounded like *yesh*.

"I'm Forrest Cohen. This is my wife Sky, and these are my daughters Venus and Earth." Forrest said. He held out his hand, but Mr. Patel just looked at it. Forrest put his hand in his pocket and waited to be invited in.

Mr. Patel looked them up and down with an angry frown on his face. He said, "Come in," then moved to the side, allowed them to enter, and he closed the door behind them. He led them through the beautifully furnished apartment into a formal dining room.

"This is my wife," Mr. Patel said.

His wife sat at the dining table next to Ishanvi. The woman's sneer unnerved Earth. The woman, with her flowing brown hair and tan skin, looked like she was once pretty.

An array of vegetarian dishes sat on the table in porcelain dishes.

Sky whispered in Forrest's ear, "I ain't eating here. They may be tryin' to poison us."

"Dinner?" Mrs. Patel asked.

"No thanks," Forrest declined. "We ate before we came."

Earth's stomach growled loudly. Sky pulled Earth close and smiled.

"Please, have a seat," Mr. Patel invited. He sat down on the other side of Ishanvi.

"I'm going to press charges! I hope that criminal daughter of yours get life in prison!" Ishanvi's irate mother screamed, breaking the uncomfortable silence of the room. The middle-aged Indian woman shook her finger across the table in Forrest and Sky's direction.

"I'm so sorry," Forrest apologized. "From my understanding, my daughter, Venus," he pointed to Venus and continued, "was defending her sister against your daughter. Your daughter has been bullying Earth for a while now. The day the fight occurred, your daughter assaulted my youngest daughter first. Ishanvi slammed a heavy door on Earth and tripped her up in front of the class. According to the other students, Ishanvi threatened to beat up both my daughters."

Venus sat directly in front of Ishanvi with a snarl on her face. Ishanvi looked down. She could not bear to look into her abuser's eyes.

"Look at her!" Ishanvi's father growled, pointing to his daughter who sat next to him nursing three broken ribs, two black eyes, a wired jaw, and a shattered ego. She had been in the hospital for three nights after Venus's beating.

"It's not our fault that your daughter can't fight!" Sky barked. "She should be a better bully!"

Forrest slapped his forehead and gave Sky the evil eye. She was only making things worse.

"Please don't press charges. I will ensure that Venus takes anger management classes to control her temper. She's been going through a lot lately. I'm sure we can work this out."

"Control your child!" Mrs. Patel howled. "She's a wild animal! Look at her staring at our girl like a rabid dog! Dog! Dog!"

"Are you calling my daughter a bitch?" Sky asked, two seconds from giving Mrs. Patel a beating worse than what Venus gave her daughter.

Venus started laughing.

Mrs. Patel hopped up and so did Sky. Forrest grabbed Sky's arm and told her to sit down. After a few pulls from her husband, she reluctantly sat down while mumbling under her breath.

Earth sat quietly watching. Her emerald eyes darted from person to person in hopes of predicting the outcome of the situation. It was amazing that all this confusion started with her.

Ishanvi looked up at Earth and mouthed, "I'm sorry."

Earth mouthed that she was sorry too.

"Calm down everyone!" Forrest coaxed. "Let's not make things worse."

"How much?" Mr. Patel, Ishanvi's father asked.

"What do you mean?" Forrest asked.

"How much are you going to give me not to press charges?" Mr. Patel asked.

"We ain't giving you a damn thang!" Sky yelped.

"Sit down!" Forrest demanded.

Sky sat down. It was rare that she heard her husband raise his voice. It sent a jolt down her spine. She was kind of turned on. She looked at Forrest, bit her bottom lip, squeezed her legs tight, and exhaled slowly.

Forrest laughed silently at his wife. She was always in his hair and he loved it. He turned his attention from his wife back to the extortionist.

"Are you willing to sign an agreement that you will not press charges or sue or pursue any other legal ramifications?" Forrest asked.

"How much?" Mr. Patel asked.

Mrs. Patel glowered. She would rather see Venus in jail.

"A semester of tuition," Forrest offered.

Mr. Patel held out his hand and Forrest shook it.

"You will hear from my lawyer in the morning," Forrest said as he stood up. "Ladies," he called. They stood up, filed in front of him, and headed out of the door.

XXII

Khalid's dorm room spun like a spinning top; the furniture moved while the room stayed in place, then came to a halt. A pale skinned man with ice blue eyes stood side by side with Turiel. The angel's hands and feet were bound by golden shackles. One of his wings was torn. His golden skin was spotted with scorch marks. Khalid appeared holding a young man by the neck like a mother dog would hold her puppies. Khalid threw the man at the feet of the pale one. Turiel stepped to Khalid's side. The shackles fell away, and his wing regenerated. A woman appeared between Khalid and the pale one. The pale one struck her down. She hit the floor and turned into a ball of light. Turiel was sucked into the light, but the light disappeared before he could become immersed. The pale one pounced on Khalid, wrapping his thin elongated fingers around his neck. Khalid's breath stopped.

Sadie sprung up in her bed. Sweat covered her face. She couldn't catch her breath. She cried out and James opened his eyes. He turned on the bedside light. Sadie's face was trembling and wet with sweat. Her nightgown clung to her body.

"What happened? You okay?" James asked.

Sadie shook her head, still unable to draw breath. She pressed her chest with one of her hands hoping to push out the air trapped in her lungs. She pulled at her neck. It felt as if the fingers that strangled her son had tried to strangle her as well.

James rubbed her back and coaxed her to inhale and to exhale slowly. She obediently followed his lead until she was able to draw breath comfortably.

"You okay, baby?" James asked, nervous to receive the answer. It had been a long time since Sadie had been awakened by nightmares and James wanted nothing to do with those perilous times.

Sadie nodded. She leaned her head into his chest and wrapped her arms and legs around him; trembling like it was zero degrees.

"What's goin' on?" James asked. "Talk to me."

"I had a bad dream," Sadie confessed.

"What was it, baby?" James asked rocking her and rubbing her arms to warm her up. He pulled the cover up to her waist.

"Khalid died. A wraith of a man killed him!" she cried.

"It was just a dream," James said as he held her. "It was just a dream. Khalid is strong and very well liked. No one wants to harm him."

Sadie knew that there was no such thing as just a dream in her family. Dreams meant something. Her son was in trouble. Her soul knew it. Her mothering instinct knew it. She just knew it.

"Something is wrong?" Sadie whimpered.

"Nothing's wrong. If it will make you feel better, I will call him in the morning and ask him if he is okay," James promised. Guilt poked at him. He didn't want to tell Sadie about Uriel seeing her mother and telling him to take care of Khalid. Selfishly, James did not want to open the door for any kind of supernatural shenanigans. He wanted to keep the peace in his home. He wanted things between him and Sadie to remain as they were.

"Maybe we should ask Uriel what Khalid had to talk to him about," Sadie suggested. "He would know if Khalid is truly okay."

"Maybe you should let me talk to 'em both and relax yo'self," James commanded. "I don't want you to make a mountain out of a molehill. Promise me that you will let me handle it."

Sadie nodded her head knowing in her heart that James would not get her the answers that she was seeking.

XX|||

Sadie's food, redolent with spices, filled the entire house. Khalid walked into the front door and greedily inhaled the scent. His girlfriend Yvette slowly walked in behind him admiring the beauty of Khalid's home. African art and bright colored paintings were everywhere. She felt like she was in a museum.

"Is that you Khalid?" Sadie yelled from the kitchen.

"Yes Ma!" Khalid yelled back. He put his keys in his pocket and closed the door behind him. It was the first time he had been home since he started school. Uriel insisted on him coming home for dinner, so they could talk.

Sadie rushed into the living room and threw her arms around her son.

"So good to see you," she said as she kissed his forehead. Sadie held on to him a little longer than usual due to the horrific dream she had about his death. The thought of someone harming her baby drove her insane.

Khalid wiped the wetness off his forehead and blushed.

Sadie looked at Yvette, surprised to see an additional guest.

Sadie greeted, "Hello. Pleasure to meet you. I'm Mrs. Tucker, Khalid's mother. You are?"

"Yvette. Nice to meet you ma'am," Yvette extended her hand, but Sadie pulled her into a hug.

"I'm a hugger," Sadie said.

Yvette reminded Sadie of Sky with her colorful clothes, excessive jewelry, and brightly colored hair. Yvette wore a rainbow-colored body dress with fruit shaped earrings and a baker's dozen of bracelets in every color. Her blonde braids completed her look. Sadie looked at her son and raised an eyebrow. He had never brought a girl home before. Maybe he was serious about this one. Sadie was happy that he had chosen someone with so much pizazz. She always assumed he would go for a more polished type like Venus.

Yvette hugged Sadie back and exhaled. Nervousness left her immediately.

"How is school going?" Sadie asked.

"It's good. I'm doing well in my classes and I may win the swim team a championship trophy," Khalid answered. "Where's dad and Uriel?"

"Your father should be here soon. He had to work late. Uriel is in his room playing video games," Sadie answered. "Have a seat. I have to get back to the kitchen. Dinner will be ready in fifteen minutes."

"Okay Mom," Khalid said as he watched her disappear from the living room. He and Yvette sat upon the couch and waited.

"Yo' mama so pretty," Yvette complimented. "She looks too young to have gray hair." She blew a big bubble gum bubble and it popped loudly. The pop echoed through the room.

"She grayed early," Khalid responded dryly. Sometimes when he looked at Yvette, all he saw was an unrefined hood rat. At other times she looked like a diamond in the rough. He couldn't decide what he saw at the moment; therefore, he questioned his decision to bring her to meet his parents. Not that his parents were snobs. They were far from it. His father was a common man and his mother was an educated woman. Neither of them had airs about themselves. Khalid, however, was of a different breed.

"Hey!" Uriel said as he walked into the room. He rushed over to Yvette to shake her hand.

"I'm Uriel," he said with a big wide grin on his face. He found her to be absolutely beautiful.

"Hi. I'm Yvette. Nice to meet you," she responded.

"Nice to meet you too," Uriel said through his upturned mouth. "I didn't know you had a girlfriend Khalid," Uriel said and lightly punched him on the arm.

"Me either," Khalid responded as he punched Uriel back, only a bit harder.

"Ouch!" Uriel laughed. "You play too much!"

Yvette crossed her arms and stuck out her bottom lip, offended by Khalid's response. Her cathexis in him heightened her insecurities daily because she felt that there was no emotional investment in her.

The front door swung open and James stepped through. He dropped his briefcase on the floor and trotted over to his oldest son. James grabbed Khalid into a bear hug, lifting him from the floor and dropping him down.

"Hey boy! What's goin' on?" James said. "Good to see you!" His stomach flipped at the half truth. Seeing Khalid was always bittersweet, and this time around it was more bitter than sweet due to Sadie's worry for him.

"Good to see you too!" Khalid said. "I missed ya'll."

"We missed you too big head!" Uriel responded.

"Who is this beautiful young thang and what in the world is she doing with you?" James asked playfully while looking at Yvette.

She blushed fifty shades of red.

"This is my friend Yvette," Khalid introduced.

James kissed her hand and said, "Very nice to meet you. Welcome to our home. Now, let's go eat!"

They walked into the dining room where Sadie had already set the table. A fresh bouquet of lavender and turquoise flowers sat in the center of the table. Dishes filled with delectable delights sat in a straight line between the plates. Sadie brought in a tray of hot rolls and sat down next to her husband. Uriel blessed the food and they all dug in.

"So, what brings you home?" James asked with his mouth full of food.

"Baby wipe your mouth," Sadie scolded.

James wiped his mouth and took a sip of wine.

"A man can't come home?" Khalid asked, laughing between bites.

"Yeah you can," James mumbled through a stuffed mouth. "But, I know you. You got a reason."

"I came to see Uriel," Khalid admitted. "I missed my brother."

"You don't miss us? I like your nerve," Sadie quipped.

"Of course, I miss you mom. I miss you the most," Khalid said blowing a kiss to his mother. "But, I came to see Uriel."

"Is everything okay?" James asked; a little worried about the visit. He recalled Uriel telling him about Khalid being afraid of his roommate.

"Yeah," Khalid answered. "Everything is good."

Uriel ate silently. He would talk to Khalid later outside of his parent's earshot. He kept his head down so that his face would not betray him.

"Tell us about yourself Yvette," Sadie asked. "Are you from Atlanta?"

"I was born in Chicago, but I grew up in St. Louis until I moved to Houston in high school," Yvette said.

"You've lived in a lot of places," Sadie observed.

"Yes. My mom and I moved around a lot. She was always running from my crazy daddy. She had to kill him for him to leave us alone," Yvette said nonchalantly before putting another fork full of food in her mouth.

Khalid shook his head slowly. He couldn't believe Yvette would divulge such information to a bunch of people she didn't know. Especially when those people were his family.

"Killed your dad?" Uriel asked. He swallowed hard and waited for her response.

"Yes. He used to beat us really bad. No matter where we moved, he always found us. The last time he found us, he broke into our house in the middle of the night and tried to attack my mom. She grabbed her gun from her nightstand and shot him," Yvette said. "I'm glad she did. He was crazy."

Sadie and James looked at one another and then at Khalid. He tried to avoid their eyes.

"How do you like school?" Sadie asked changing the subject. There was nothing she could think to say regarding the murder of Yvette's father.

Before she could answer, Khalid got up from the table and asked Uriel to follow him. He reluctantly left Yvette to talk to his parents. There was no telling what she would say next.

Khalid and Uriel went into their bedroom and sat down on the beds. Uriel got up and closed the door.

"What's up?" Uriel asked. "What took you so long to come over?"

"I was busy. Did you get any insight on my roommate?" Khalid asked.

"I did. I prayed about your roommate and God gave me a dream. I dreamed that there is something inside of him and beside him. Like he is possessed by something and that thing has a friend. The demon is killing your roommate. The thing inside of him is very old and very evil. Stay away from him Khalid. He means you harm," Uriel warned.

Khalid sat in quiet contemplation for a moment then asked, "I met a girl. She says that she was sent to help me. Who is she?"

"I'm not sure, but in that same dream I saw a woman standing behind you helping you fight that thing inside your roommate. She was not strong enough," Uriel said. "I don't really understand what the dream means. All I know is that you should stay away from him. He wants to trade with you. Don't do it."

"Thanks for your help," Khalid said. He felt like he had wasted his gas driving all the way home. Uriel had not told him anything he didn't know already. It was obvious that Belial was evil. That didn't bother Khalid because he felt evil was relative. Some may have considered him evil. Khalid was disappointed that the strange girl would be of little assistance and he had already decided to look inside of Belial's box, but Khalid could not imagine anything Belial may have wanted to trade.

"You're welcome," Uriel said. "I know you won't listen to me but be careful. Okay?"

"Okay," Khalid answered. "Let's go eat." He stood up to leave.

"Okay," Uriel paused. "Did I tell you I saw Mama C?"

Khalid's heart stopped beating. He dropped back down onto the bed like something pushed him.

"Why would you say that?" Khalid asked.

"Because I saw her. I saw her twice. She told me to take care of you," Uriel said.

Khalid nodded and left the room. He didn't want to hear anymore. The death of his grandmother was the most devastating event of his young life and Khalid refused to sit with his brother talking about messages beyond the grave.

Uriel followed behind. He touched his brother's shoulder, but Khalid shook away Uriel's hand.

The brothers rejoined the family in the dining room and fellowshipped until it was time for Khalid and Yvette to go back to school.

XXIV

"What's going on with you?" Yvette whispered; sitting across the table from Khalid in the middle of the crowded university library.

Midterm exams were coming, and students were cramming. Books, highlighters, paper, pens, and laptops cluttered each table. The sound of typing, whispering, and turning pages set the room abuzz.

"I don't have time for this," Khalid whispered back. He flipped through the pages of a book and ran his bright yellow highlighter across the page.

"Just tell me what's wrong. Did I do something? You've been acting funny since I met your family," Yvette said.

Khalid kept reading as if he didn't hear a thing.

"Khalid!" she spat between her teeth causing wetness to hit Khalid's hand. He looked up with eyes narrowed and full of disdain. He looked at her like an anathema.

"I'm sorry," she said. She leaned back in her chair.

"Didn't I tell you that I didn't have time for this? Don't you see me studying?" he growled.

"You don't need to study. School is easy for you. Just talk to me," Yvette begged.

"What do you want me to say? If I tell you the truth you will cry like you always do," Khalid said.

"What did I do?" she asked again.

"Where do I begin?" he asked, leaning back. His eyes were so intense that chills ran down her back. He continued, "Your self-esteem is disgusting. You follow me around like a lovesick puppy knowing that I sleep around freely and often. I invite you to my parent's home and you horrify them with tales of your family's supreme dysfunction. Your clownish appearance is a deterrent to most, but I appreciate a challenge. You're beautiful. I can give you that, but the verdict is still out on your degree of intelligence."

Yvette sat with her arms crossed tight across her chest. Her lips began trembling. The tears came.

"See," Khalid said. "This is why I didn't want to talk. You forced me to be cruel."

"I love you," Yvette cried. "Why are you doing this? Please don't leave me."

Khalid laughed.

Yvette's silent tears became an audible whimper.

"We're not a couple Yvette," Khalid stated. "I am not ending our friendship. There is no need to cry."

Khalid reached across the table and placed his hand upon her arm. The warmth of his hand sent electricity through her. She became drunk by his touch. She hopped up and ran around the table and plopped herself right into his lap. Yvette kissed him deeply and hugged him tightly. It was insane how a boy who was two years younger than her could make her crazy.

Khalid kissed her back then pulled away.

"Go sit down," he instructed.

Yvette went back to her seat and opened her book. Tears still streamed down her face, but she refused to give credence to their presence.

Khalid picked up his highlighter and began where he left off. A light tap on his shoulder caused him to look up. Hafeeza stood behind him.

"Hello again," she said as she pulled a chair to the table.

Yvette's eyes stretched wide. She couldn't believe the nerve of the strange woman. It was common knowledge around campus that Yvette didn't like any female near her man.

"This table is full," Yvette said.

Hafeeza completely ignored Yvette and sat down placing her books right next to Khalid's.

"Hello," Khalid responded.

Yvette looked at him like she wanted to pull his face from his skull.

"Khalid, who is this ugly ho?" Yvette screeched. Yvette pushed back from the table getting ready to fight.

"Calm down," Khalid said with a warning glare. "And don't be rude! Apologize."

"Sorry," she mumbled.

"I didn't hear you," Khalid scolded.

"Sorry," Yvette yelled.

Hafeeza ignored her completely.

Yvette angrily sulked in her seat.

"What do you want?" Khalid asked Hafeeza, whose eyes were burrowing into Khalid's.

"To warn you," she said. "Do not accept his offer."

"What are you talking about?" he asked.

"The ancient one," she said, gathering her books and leaving.

Khalid and Yvette watched as Hafeeza quickly exited the building.

"She's weird as hell," Yvette mumbled under her breath.

"You have no idea," Khalid agreed and continued his studies, but he couldn't help but to wonder about the deal he had been warned about now for a second time.

XXV

Hartsfield-Jackson Airport was always busy. People of every creed and color milled around the airport. Flights boarded and landed what seemed like every minute of the day. Being the busiest airport in the world was an understatement. Specialty shops lined the lobby along with a variety of restaurants and magazine stands.

Forrest grabbed his bag from baggage claim and made his way to the passenger pick-up area. Before he could pull out his cell phone, he heard his name being called. Forrest looked up and saw his two best friends waving from a distance.

"James! Luis!" Forrest exclaimed. He greeted both men with a handshake and pulled them in for a hug.

"It's been a while," Luis said with a thick New York Puerto Rican accent. He had been in Atlanta for over twenty years, yet he sounded like he still lived deep within the Bronx.

"Yes, it has," Forrest agreed.

It had been eight years since Forrest had seen James and Luis together. Luis visited New York three years prior and Forrest was able to catch up with him then. James visited New York five years ago. Their meeting was pleasant but odd because of their shared unease stemming from the events that happened in Atlanta before the Cohens returned to New York.

"How was your flight?" James asked as they walked out of the airport to the parking garage.

The three piled into James's car and exited the airport onto the highway.

"Where're you stayin'? Luis asked from the back seat. His curly hair was cut into a short fade. His t-shirt read, *F You. Pay me.*

"At the Four Seasons," Forrest answered feeling guilty. He always stayed with one of his friends when he visited, but this time he felt too uncomfortable to stay with anyone. Forrest was emotionally drained and had very little desire to share his space. He needed privacy to cuss, scream, and cry if he needed to.

"You love to spend money," Luis responded. "You are welcome to stay with me. I have plenty of room. Me and my wife just bought a new house."

"Your wife?" James and Forrest yelled in unison.

"When did you get married?" James asked. "Why didn't you tell us?"

"I eloped about a month ago. It happened in Vegas; spur of the moment," Luis said, leaning back and pulling his cell phone out of his pocket. He pulled a picture up and passed the phone to Forrest.

"She's hot!" Forrest yelped and showed the picture to James when he was able to stop at a red light.

The woman in the picture was a full-figured woman with dark chocolate skin, large eyes and lips, medium length twists in her hair, and a pearly white smile.

"What's her name?" James asked; a smirk on his face. He was simply floored that Luis had gotten married. Luis always said he would never get married. Women were necessary evils to him. The spider had been caught by the fly.

"Shaka," Luis answered licking his lips. "Royalty like Shaka Zula. She's my queen. She got the key to the kingdom."

"How did this happen?" Forrest asked. "I thought no chick would ever tie you down!" he laughed. "She must have put it on you!"

"Whatever man," Luis barked. "She cool. She makes me better."

"How so?" Forrest asked.

"I wanna be a better man when I'm wit' her. She encourages me to chase my dreams and make a brotha feel like I'm the king of the world. She believes in me. I never had that. She everything," Luis answered honestly.

"Congratulations man. I'm happy for you," James said, still shaking his head. He could not believe Luis had gotten married. Luis had been anti-marriage his entire life. James knew that Shaka must be one special lady to convert Luis.

"Me too," Forrest agreed. "I wish you forever."

"Thanks," Luis grumbled. All the love talk was making him uncomfortable. "So how long you gone be here?" he asked Forrest.

"A week. Sky wants me to look at a few places. She wants to move back to Atlanta," said Forrest.

"Really?" Luis asked. "After all the drama she been through, she wants to come back here? That chick crazy!"

"Whatcha mouth," Forrest spat. Honestly, he felt the same way. He couldn't understand why Sky would ever want to return to Atlanta. Atlanta had been nothing but a place of horror and pain for his wife. If it was up to him, he would never step foot in the city again.

James said nothing. He was loath to participate in the conversation because he knew that Luis and Forrest blamed Sadie for all that had happened in the past.

"Why she wanna come back?" Luis asked.

"She wants to be near Sadie," Forrest answered, trying to decide if the time was right to tell Luis about Sky's illness.

"That's weird. Them chicks too close if you ask me," Luis said in his usual combative tone.

"No one asked you," Forrest snapped back. "Why are you always trying to stir up trouble?"

"I speak the truth!" Luis said. "It is weird if your wife wants to uproot the life of her whole family to be next to another woman. Sadie and Sky are too liberated for their own good. Ya'll sleepin'. Next thing you know they gone be divorcing both of ya'll to marry each other."

James couldn't keep his silence anymore. He began to laugh sadly.

"You are too stupid for your own good," Forrest responded shaking his head.

"Why she want to come back to Atlanta then?" Luis asked with one eyebrow raised.

"Sky has stage four cancer. The doctor says that she can die at any time," Forrest answered.

He looked out of the window in case the tear he so desperately tried to prevent from forming appeared and made its way down his cheek.

Luis's mouth dropped open. He put his hand on Forrest's shoulder and said, "I'm sorry. Please forgive me. I was just talkin' trash."

"I know," Forrest said. "No hard feelings."

Luis leaned back in his seat. Sadness filled him. He liked Sky. She was cool. He admired her sassy nature.

"The kids know?" Luis asked.

"Yes," Forrest answered.

"How they takin' it?" asked James.

"I'm not sure. I don't think Mars really understands. The oldest ones are quiet about it. They haven't said anything. Venus got into a bad fight. She beat a girl so badly that we had to pay off her parents, so they wouldn't press charges," said Forrest. "Earth stays in her room a lot and Jupiter keeps himself busy. I think they think if they don't talk about it, the cancer will go away."

"How's Sky takin' it?" Luis asked. "Stop right here," he told James as they drove near a gas station.

James pulled into the station. Luis jumped out of the car and ran inside to get a six pack of beer. There was no way he was going to finish the conversation sober. Luis bought his beer and returned to the car. The men pulled back into traffic.

"I'm sorry," Luis said. "How Sky takin' it?"

"Not good," Forrest answered. "Not good at all. All she talks about is missing our children grow up and if I will eventually get them a new mother."

"That's sad dude?" said Luis. He took a big gulp of beer and offered one to his friends, but they declined. "So, you gonna stay with me and my queen?"

"Naw. My room is prepaid and I kinda want to be alone. I feel like I have not slept since I found out," Forrest confessed. "I need time to download my thoughts, but we all can hang while I'm here and ya'll can help me look around for a new house."

"I understand," Luis said. "We gotcha back."

"Wanna go straight to the hotel or what?" James asked before he passed the exit for the hotel.

"I'm hungry," Forrest said.

"Me too," agreed Luis.

"Then, we gone eat!" James said as he pushed the gas petal and sped off down the highway.

XXVI

A noise woke Khalid from his sleep. His eyes opened slowly. A shadow hovered over him, dark and see-through but in full human form. He sprang to his feet with feline agility. The shadow shifted and fell behind its master who was standing a foot in front of Khalid.

"Good morning," Belial said, his breath infiltrating Khalid's nose like a gas bomb thrown by the police.

"Good morning," Khalid answered, his chiseled chest sweating and heaving. He pulled on a T-shirt, so he would not feel half naked standing there in his boxer briefs. He looked at the clock. It read 3:33 am.

"I'm sorry to disturb you," Belial apologized. "I was meditating, and somehow got beside myself." A smile split his face in two.

"Stay the hell away from me man!" Khalid huffed. "I'm not playing games no more!" He confronted Belial, literally face to face. Belial exhaled and the stench from his mouth sent Khalid stumbling backward.

Belial laughed. He said, "Calm down my friend. There is no need to be upset. I meant you no harm." He pulled out his desk chair and sat in it. "Please, have a seat." Belial pointed to Khalid's bed.

Khalid sat down.

"Who are you?" Khalid asked. It was painfully obvious that Belial was not just a weird college kid. He was something frightening and somewhat familiar. Something about his eyes told a story that was primeval and raw.

"A very old associate of your father. More like a half-brother or distant cousin one may say," he said. "You can say that we fell to earth together."

Khalid leaned backward. The breath of the man turned Khalid's stomach inside out. It smelled like death.

"What are you talking about?" Khalid spat.

He looked at the pale skinny man, with a map of blue veins under his translucent flesh, up and down. He was not beautiful like Turiel. His smell was not pleasant. No light beamed from his orifices. There was no way he could have been an angel; even a fallen one.

"We were Watchers. Holy ones send to watch over the creations of God," he grumbled. "If your grandfather was alive, he would have referenced the Dead Sea Scrolls, Book of Jubilees, the Damascus Documents, and all kinds of foolish documents that think they know the history of me!"

"You know nothing of my grandfather," Khalid spat.

"I know you killed him," Belial cackled. "You killed him like you killed many others who got in your way."

"I was a baby," Khalid mumbled.

He was a newborn in his mother's arms when his grandfather dropped dead.

"Your soul, like mine, was never a baby," Belial retorted. "We are the chaos that God tried to bring order to during creation."

Khalid sulked silently. He knew it was true. He waited for his roommate to finish talking. Khalid considered killing him after the conversation was over. It would be pleasurable to feel the skin of Belial's scrawny neck locked tight within Khalid's large hands.

"In the beginning, all was well. I was respected, revered, and even worshiped. I was called The King of Evil, Prince of Darkness, the Father of Necromancy and Sorcery. I gave the children of earth power. I showed them how to use the elements to get what they desired instead of praying to the one who never answers! I was the ruler of this world until the Ancient of Days decided that I was a thorn in His side. I was no longer a balance to the universe but a nuisance to be stamped out. My sons of darkness fell victim to the Angels of Light. My followers dispersed like the cowards they were. We were cast down into the pit! Blah blah blah blah!" Belial grumbled, anger distorting his face more and more. "I was demoted to the worthless one; my followers to the sons of worthlessness!"

"I don't believe you," Khalid said as a matter of fact. "You are nothing more than a goth white boy with a vivid imagination who is in desperate need of a breath mint."

Belial smirked and said, "You don't really believe that. I have been called the Father of Lies, but that title does not rightfully belong to me."

"If you are who you say you are, where is my father?" Khalid asked.

"He has been where he has always been; watching," Belial waved his hand in a circle and let his eyes follow in a circular motion. The arm of his shadow did not move at all.

"What is that thing?" Khalid asked, the hairs on his arms standing up.

"One of my children. A son of darkness," Belial answered. He stood up and twirled around, his shadow followed three steps behind with most movements contrary to its master's.

"Why are you here?" Khalid asked. He kept his eyes on the shadow as it settled behind Belial when he sat back in his chair.

"To make a trade," Belial answered. "You have something I want. I have something you want."

"I don't think so," Khalid replied. There was nothing that Khalid could conceive of wanting from his possessed roommate.

"I have your father trapped in my box. He's waiting for you to set him free," Belial cooed.

Anger began to fill Khalid from the bottom of his feet to his scalp. Hot tears ran down the corner of his eyes.

"You lie!" Khalid belted. "I do not feel him near. I have not felt him near me since he was banished from my parent's house. If he were near, I would smell him. I would feel him. He would talk to me!"

"Did you not smell him upon the breath of the fairies?" Belial asked. "Did you not see them carry his light? I know you felt him. I could see it in your eyes. You lie!" Belial laughed. "You lie to yourself silly boy!"

Khalid's grimace softened. He remembered smelling myrrh when the light beings flew around Belial that night. He remembered the feeling of familiarity in their song.

"Where is he?" Khalid asked.

"Like I told you, he's in my box," said Belial.

Khalid didn't believe him. He didn't believe that Belial knew his father. Belial was probably a demon, and not a very powerful one at that, who needed Khalid to do something for him. Khalid had read about such entities during his study of the occult. If Belial had any real power, he would not be lurking around a college campus posing as a student. He was worthless.

"Let me see him," Khalid said, one of his eyebrows rose.

"You have to open the box," Belial said.

"Why can't you open it?" Khalid asked.

"I can, but I can't release Turiel. Only you can," Belial said.

"Why is that?" Khalid asked suspiciously.

"Because you are his and he is yours," Belial answered.

"What does that mean?" Khalid inquired.

Belial replied, "Exactly what I said. You are his offspring and he is your father. As his progeny, you have the power to release him."

Khalid remained quiet for a moment hoping for further explanation. None came.

"What do I have to do?" Khalid asked annoyed by the sound of Belial's voice, his enigmatic babbling, and his putrid breath. Speaking with Belial was worse than thin fingernails bending backward.

"Cut your finger and run it over the markings on the box. Call your father's name and he will come," Belial answered.

"What do you want?" Khalid asked.

"A new body," Belial admitted. "As you can smell, this one is deteriorating." Belial handed Khalid a student ID with a picture of a rosy cheeked, handsome young man. The name on the ID read Austin Underdue. He looked identical to Belial without the translucent skin, strange eyes, and disgusting teeth.

Khalid gasped in horror. The thought of a demon taking over some poor kid's body made him want to vomit. He remembered how it was when Turiel took over his grandmother. He wondered what Austin Underdue's family was going through. They probably thought their son was having a mental breakdown.

"You can't have mine!" Khalid exclaimed.

Belial laughed.

"I do not want your body as nice as it may be," Belial smiled while allowing his eyes to float across Khalid from head to toe. He continued, "But, I do need a strong body. I am growing weak in this vessel. I can no longer lure someone to me to make the switch. I have become unpleasant to the eye. You must bring me someone; dead or alive."

"I can find you someone," Khalid agreed. The price was something he was willing to pay. There were plenty of college students that Khalid felt lived pointless lives.

"I get to pick him," Belial said.

"Him? No girls?" Khalid asked a bit amused.

Belial's face twisted. He answered "No! Women are way too complicated and very difficult to possess."

Khalid's idea of giving him Yvette flew out the window. He held out his hand. Belial shook it and the agreement was struck.

"Now, let's bring daddy home," Belial cackled as he picked up a knife and slit Khalid's fingertip.

XVII

Sky bounced her bottom in the kitchen while wearing a Wonder Woman apron and stirring a big pot of sauce. Her bare feet danced across the floor to music blaring African drums. Voices sang in languages unknown but known deep within the ancestral soul. Her hips wiggled, and her fingers snapped between each stir, chop, and dash of seasoning.

It felt good to dance. Dancing always made her world better. She pulled the rubber band from her hair and let her kinky, curly locks fly like a war banner.

Jupiter walked into the dining room and watched from behind the counter. He smiled. It was good to see his mother happy. He had not seen her happy since she received a death sentence. The way she moved reminded him of how she used to dance every Saturday afternoon before she sat down to write. Sky would put on her music and moved as if someone in heaven above was controlling her motion. Soon the entire family would be dancing around in a circle. Her movements drew them like magnets. Her rhythm was hypnotic; her joy hard to resist. It was nice to see her dance again. Since she had received news of cancer, she had not danced at all.

Sky looked up and saw her oldest son smiling at her. She held out her hand for him to join her. Without hesitation, he was spinning her around and moving his hips to the rhythm of his ancestors.

Earth and Venus peeked into the kitchen and were asked to join in. They did. Sky called for Mars and he too joined the stomping, spinning, hip shaking, and hopping. Laughter permeated the air mingling with Sky's melodious voice singing her love for her children. They danced until sweat formed in their armpits and behind their knees. They sang and laughed until their throats hurt. They gyrated until their stomach muscles ached.

Behind Sky, her mother appeared. She wore the robes of her people. She danced the Ekombi dance of happiness and beauty. Her feet moved in intricate motions as her hips moved like the waves of the ocean. Earth began to mimic her grandmother. Earth's hips moved as if she had known the dance her entire life. Graceful movements flowed through her entire body. Her mother and siblings took notice.

"Earth," Sky called. "How did you learn to do that?"

"Grandma is teaching her," Mars answered as he stared off behind his mother trying to replicate the moves himself. "Grandma has been teaching us lots of things since you have been sick."

An eerie feeling gathered in Sky's chest. She remembered her mother always saying that the dead will gather the dead. Sky hadn't seen her mother yet, so maybe death was not as close as she thought.

Sky's mother danced, and Earth followed.

Sky and Jupiter stopped, and watched in awe of the spectacle before them.

Venus stopped dancing. A frown pulled her mouth open. She yelled, "Why ya'll always have to ruin stuff with all that spooky talk! Grandma ain't here! Grandma is dead!

She was dead before we were born! Mom make them stop telling lies!"

Venus pushed Mars to the side and grabbed Earth's arm so hard that fingernail prints imprinted her skin.

"Stop!" Venus yelled. "I don't want to hear about dead people! When mom dies, are ya'll going to see her too!"

Earth stopped moving and started to cry. Mars cried with her.

"Grandma is right there!" Mars wailed. "We aren't lying! Can you see her mom?"

Sky shook her head no. It was true; she could not see her mother, but the scent of her mother lingered in the air.

"I hate you!" Venus belted; her brown face turning into a red bubble. "If you don't stop crying, I'm going to kill you both!"

Sky grabbed hold of Venus and pulled her into a tight hug. She kissed the top of her daughter's head and rocked her in her arms. The flood gates opened, and Venus wailed until her voice thundered through every room.

"Don't die Mama. Please don't die!" Venus cried. "I can't live without you!"

Jupiter wrapped his arms around Venus and Sky. Earth and Mars threw their arms around their older siblings.

"You can't leave me!" Venus wailed. "Whose gonna take care of us and Daddy?"

"Shh, baby," Sky soothed. "I will always be here no matter what," she promised. She adjusted her arms until they were wrapped around all her children. Tears began to fall upon the tops of their heads as she felt a pair of invisible arms wrap around her. Sky knew instantly, that the familiar hug was from her mother.

XVIII

Pain surged through Khalid's finger as his blood poured over the ancient inscriptions carved into Belial's box. Belial held Khalid's finger like a pencil, tracing each marking carefully. Blood transformed into light as Khalid's finger moved across the box. After the last symbol was touched, the box sprang open and the humming light forces flew out of the box knocking Khalid backward. He hit the floor bottom first; his eyes affixed on the flying creatures circling Belial.

"Call him forth," Belial said. "Call his name!"

Khalid climbed to his knees and yelled, "Turiel!"

The light forces circled faster flying high and low in an elliptical motion.

"Turiel, I command you to appear to me. Father come!" Khalid cried out.

A bright light shot from the box momentarily filling the room with a blinding glare. Turiel appeared, hands and feet bound in gold shackles. One of his wings was torn and his skin looked scorched. His robes were tattered, and his angelic luster was gone. His head hung as if each strand of his hair weighed a ton. The light forces encircled him then lined his shoulders like lightening bugs sitting on leaves.

"Father!" Khalid cried, flummoxed to see the angelic creature brought low.

The angel looked at him with eyes wrecked with pain.

"Who did this to you?" Khalid wailed.

Turiel opened his mouth but nothing came out. Khalid observed a thin golden collar around Turiel's neck.

"There, there boy," Belial cackled. "You ask too many questions."

"Let him go!" Khalid yelled.

"Not until you give me your half of the bargain," Belial responded, his shadow standing beside him stroking the curly hair of the angel.

"Don't let that thing touch him!" Khalid belched.

He got up from the floor and darted over to his father.

The shadow shifted places and appeared behind its owner.

"I will bring you a new body. Trust me. I am a man of my word. You have to remove those shackles. He's in pain," Khalid requested.

"I can't do that," said Belial; arms crossed and shaking his head. "But, what I will do is let him remain out of the box. He can stay in the room with us until you bring me a body."

"Take the pain away from him," Khalid commanded "or the deal is off!"

"Very well," Belial agreed.

He waved his hand and the light beings perched on Turiel's shoulder flew up into the air like a band of shooting stars. They began to circle Turiel. Tiny bits of light rained upon the angel like glitter and stuck to his skin giving him back his angelic luster. The dark spots on Turiel's skin faded away into brilliant gold. The angel lifted his head. His eyes were no longer stressed. His broken wing regenerated as if an invisible hand was stitching it back together.

"How about his voice?" Khalid asked.

"No can do," Belial said. "Words hold power. I have done all that I am going to do for now. Bring me a body and your father will be free."

Belial waved his hand again and the light beings flew back into the box. The box slammed shut behind them. Khalid's blood markings dissolved into the wood leaving no trace.

"I must go to class. I suggest you purchase a cot for him. He will soon grow tired of standing," Belial jested as he and his shadow exited the dorm room.

X|X

"How was Atlanta?" Jupiter asked his father as Forrest unpacked his suitcase and threw his clothes in the laundry basket. He had just got home from the airport and was anxious to take a shower and climb into bed. He wondered where his wife and daughters were. It was odd for the house to be so quiet. Usually Venus was blasting music or Earth was reading her poetry aloud in the mirror Jupiter was dribbling a basketball through the house or Mars was laughing hysterically while watching cartoons or Sky would be listening to her books being read back to her by the text to voice software on her computer. It was one of the ways that she edited her writing, but these days the computer voice reading from her laptop had been swapped out for eerie TV shows and internet videos.

"Where are the ladies?" Forrest asked.

"Out shopping for dinner. Mars is in his room asleep," Jupiter answered.

"Okay. Atlanta was cool. I got to spend time with my friends and look at some neighborhoods," answered Forrest. "The city has changed so much. New apartment buildings are going up everywhere."

"How were Uncle James and Uncle Luis?" asked Jupiter. He called them uncle because they were the closest men that his father had for brothers.

"Both of them are doing well. Luis just got married," said Forrest. "James is thinking about retiring."

"I can't believe Uncle Luis got married. He seemed not to like women very much. I kinda thought he was gay," Jupiter admitted.

Forrest laughed aloud.

"That's funny," Forrest said. "I'm going to tell him you said that. What happened while I was gone?"

"Venus spazzed out because Mars and Earth claimed that they saw grandma dancing in the kitchen. Other than that, Mom is doing okay. We missed you Dad," Jupiter said. He sat on the fainting couch at the end of Forrest's bed and asked, "Are we moving to Atlanta?"

"Maybe," said Forrest. "Your mother wants to. I'm not so sure. I missed all of you too."

"I want to move too," Jupiter said. "I'm tired of the cold."

Forrest looked up at his oldest son a bit surprised. He thought Jupiter loved New York. Jupiter consistently wore New York street gear. He was immersed in the art scene, hip hop culture, literary scene, and political scene. Jupiter took pride representing New York City. Forrest thought Jupiter would be his ally against moving to Atlanta, now it was clear that Forrest was on his own.

"Why?" Forrest asked. "You've never shown any interest in Atlanta."

"Mom would be happier there and so would Venus and Earth. They are really close to Auntie Sadie's kids. Everyone is struggling up here. I want mom's last days to be happy," Jupiter admitted. A tear caused him to see a kaleidoscope of color through his red eyelashes.

"How about you?" Forrest asked. He sat down next to his son and put his arm around him. "What will make you happy?"

"I just want mom to be happy. Happiness makes people live longer. That's a scientific fact. I can thrive anywhere. I'm a powerful black man," he said in a deep voice mimicking James Earl Jones.

Forrest began to laugh. Seeing his pale, red headed son call himself a powerful black man tickled him to the core. He said, "I here you brother. In that case, Atlanta may be a perfect place for you. Maybe for all of us."

XXX

Sadie sat in her home office twiddling her thumbs. The dream she had about Khalid had been nagging her like a bad tooth ache. She couldn't get the images out of her mind. They tortured her psyche night and day.

Sadie picked up her cell phone and put it down again. She didn't know who to call. James didn't want to hear anything else about the dream. Sadie was afraid to tell Sky because she did not want anything to deter Sky from moving back to Atlanta, and hearing about Sadie's dream would certainly cause Forrest to refuse to move. Times like this, Sadie missed her father the most. Not only would Mr. Covington understand, he would help with a possible solution. He would find the meaning of the dream, and make sure things were handled in the best possible way. Talking to the nuns she worked for was out of the question. Last time she tried that, all she was offered was prayer.

Sadie picked up her phone again and began to scroll through her contacts. The first name she saw was Ari Aniwodi-El. She half smiled. He was one of the only men who ever gave her butterflies. Something about his eyes always made her feel like a school girl. Sadie used to innocently enjoy their chemistry. She had not spoken to Dr. Aniwodi-El since he helped exorcise her mother eight years prior. After that experience, he respectfully asked Sadie to never call him again, and so far, she had respected his request.

Sadie put the phone down. She placed her head in her hands and took a few deep breaths. Sadie picked the phone up again and pressed call.

"Hello," Dr. Ari Aniwodi-El answered.

"Hi Ari. It's Sadie," she said as happy as she could fake.

"Sadie Tucker?" he asked a bit surprised to hear her voice. He thought he had made himself clear that he didn't want to ever speak to her again the last time they spoke.

"Yes," she answered nervously. She could tell by the tone of his voice that he was very shocked to hear from her. She instantly regretted calling. "How are you?"

"Great and you?" he answered. "How are things?"

"James and I are doing well after a rough number of years. Uriel likes school, although he struggles a bit. Khalid is off to college and loves it. How about you and your beautiful family?" Sadie asked.

"We're great. We just returned from an African safari. It was an incredible experience. I'm glad to hear that your family is doing well. How is Sky?" asked Ari.

"She's not doing so well," Sadie answered. "She was diagnosed with cancer."

"I'm so sorry to hear that. With the right treatment, cancer doesn't have to be a death sentence. Please let her know that my family will keep her in our prayers," he said.

"I will," Sadie responded after a long pause.

"So, why did you call me?" Ari asked; eager to get to the point. "I thought we agreed that it was best for our families to part ways."

"I'm sorry," Sadie said, her voice trembling. "I didn't know who else to call."

"What's wrong?" Ari asked. His instincts told him to hang up the phone, but his fondness for her was always undeniable. There was no way he could hang up when she needed his ear so badly.

"I had a terrible dream about my oldest son. I was hoping that you could shed some light on it for me. Help me understand what it means. That's all," Sadie replied. "I promise to never call you again."

"You said that eight years ago," Ari joked.

Sadie laughed halfheartedly.

Ari leaned back in his chair and pulled his waist length dreadlocks into a ponytail. He wanted to get as comfortable as possible. He prayed that his wife didn't pop by his office while he was on the phone with Sadie. His wife would be furious.

"I'm listening," he said.

Sadie exhaled a breath that she felt like she was holding for ten minutes. She was sure he was not going to give her his ear. Thank goodness she was wrong.

"I dreamed that Turiel was in Khalid's dorm room in chains. The angel was scorched. One of his wings was torn. Khalid was fighting a pale white man with long fingers. Khalid was choked to death," Sadie recounted.

Ari sat quietly trying to make sense of the images. After a few moments he said, "Images of broken wings and chains symbolize loss of freedom. Dying in a dream usually represents killing off an aspect of yourself. Maybe he is trying to liberate himself from some inner turmoil. I assume,

Khalid being who he is, must have many internal struggles. As his mother, your intuition is tapping into his emotions. Has any unnatural things occurred?"

"Nothing at all. For the first time in forever, we've been like a normal family," Sadie answered.

"Sadie, sometimes dreams are just a clearing of our subconscious. They don't always have profound meanings. Enjoy your family. I'm sure Khalid is fine," Ari said.

He felt guilty for oversimplifying the situation because he knew her family's situation was anything but simple. Her son was the seed of a fallen angel. Khalid's purpose on earth was yet to be seen, judging from the past, his purpose may be to bring chaos and disorder to the world.

Sadie knew that her dream meant more, but Ari was not willing to investigate further so she thanked him for his time and said goodbye. As soon as they hung up the phone, Ari's wife sent Sadie a text that read, "Never contact us again. God be with you and your family."

XXXI

After a long, chaotic day, the school was finally student-free. Luis did his last round around the premises to make sure all the doors were locked, and everyone was gone. Everything was copasetic. He took off his blazer and threw it over his arm, and slowly made his way to his office.

Being a middle school principal was more than he had bargained for, but he loved the work. For years he worked for social services. Six years ago, he transitioned into teaching and now he was a first-year principal. The teachers and students alike liked him for his straight talk, relatable personality, and desire to see everyone succeed. Luis always went above and beyond for his students and his teachers. It was evident that he truly cared. Coming from an impoverished background gave him a perspective that his students deeply appreciated. He was in a good place professionally and personally.

Luis sat in his office finishing up some last-minute paperwork before he headed home.

On his desk were a small stack of papers and folders, and a picture of his new wife. Luis looked at the picture and smiled. She was the best thing that had ever happened to him. Thinking about how he adored her made him think of how much Forrest adored Sky. His heart bled for him. Anticipating the death of a loved one was probably worse than death itself. Luis remembered the devastation that his grandfather experienced when his grandmother died; how he took care of her for ten years before her passing while she was virtually immobile and unable to do anything for herself. Luis's grandfather sat by her side, bathed her, fed her, and prayed over her until she drew her last breath, and although he knew death was coming, her passing shattered him still.

Luis picked up his cell and called Forrest.

Forrest answered after the second ring.

"What's up?" Forrest asked; his voice scratchy and low.

Luis couldn't decipher whether Forrest was sleeping or had lost his voice.

Luis answered, "Nothin'. Just finishing up at school. I'm getting' ready to head home. Imma get a bite to eat."

"Yeah? What are you going to eat?" Forrest answered.

"Not sure," Luis answered. He put away a few files, then picked up his keys and walked out of the school.

It was a nice day. Not too cool. Not too hot. Luis decided to roll down his windows instead of turning on the air conditioner. Outside air always felt better than inside air. He turned on some Otis Redding and allowed the raspy sound of his voice to wash the stress of the day away.

"Maybe you should get some fried chicken," Forrest answered. "I haven't had fried chicken in ages."

"Shaka got me off meat for a while. I think Imma hit up the vegetarian restaurant up the street," Luis answered.

Forrest started laughing.

"Shut up," Luis laughed. "Don't say nothin' about my woman or my diet."

"She really has your nose open. I have to meet this woman. I hate that I missed her when I was in Atlanta," Forrest said.

"She was so busy. You'll have plenty of time to meet her next time," Luis said as he pulled into the parking lot of the vegetarian restaurant. "She can't wait to go on a triple date with you and James and your wives."

Forrest had nothing to say. He wasn't sure if he was coming to Atlanta or not. He considered Jupiter's opinion on the matter, but his instincts told him that Atlanta was not where they should be.

Luis ordered his food quickly and sat down.

"Cat got yo' tongue?" Luis asked through a mouth full of kale salad. "Why you get quiet when I asked you about Atlanta?"

"I don't know if I want to move there," Forrest confessed. "I'm not sure if it's safe for my family."

"I live in Atlanta and ain't nothin' ever happened to me," Luis snapped. "What does your wife want?"

"Stop acting like you are unaware of all the crazy stuff that Sky experienced with Sadie and her family. You have seen some of it with your own eyes. You remember the time James called us over to Sadie's house before they got married? We thought he went crazy and beat her up."

"You thought that," Luis retorted. "I knew James could never do anything like that."

Forrest felt guilty for doubting his friend. That night he was ready to call the police on James without even hearing his side of the story. Sadie was in such bad shape, like she had been trapped in a torture chamber for weeks and left to die. What was Forrest supposed to think? It was difficult for him to understand how Luis gave James the benefit of a doubt.

Forrest asked, "Remember how her body was smoldering and bruised and it healed right before our eyes?"

"I remember," Luis answered while taking a sip of lemon water.

"Well, if you remember, stop acting like my concerns aren't valid!" Forrest angrily snapped.

"I didn't say your concerns weren't valid. I'm just pointin' out that Atlanta is not a dangerous place. Ain't yo' wife sick? Is she dyin'?" Luis asked.

"Yes," Forrest whispered.

"What does she want again?" Luis asked.

"She wants to leave New York," Forrest said.

"How do your children feel about movin' here?" Luis asked.

"They're down for whatever." Forrest said. "But, I don't want anything to happen to Sky dealing with Sadie."

"That was a long time ago," Luis said. "Sky was never hurt. Sadie and her family were the ones who suffered. I understand your hesitancy, but your wife is dyin' and she deserves to be around the people who love her the most."

"We love her the most," Forrest belted. "No one loves her more than me."

"If you love her, let her live her last days where she wants to. Time is too precious to waste. Tomorrow ain't promised. What if she died in the middle of this Atlanta debate? How would you feel then?"

Forrest said nothing because he knew that the guilt would do him in if that happened.

"Bro, I understand why you don't want to be down here. Ya'll been through a lot with Sadie and her family, but now ain't the time to burn bridges. This is the time to build bridges and make sure there are no hard feelings between anyone," Luis said.

Forrest knew that Luis was right.

Forrest replied, "When did you get so wise? All that reality TV you've watched must have taught you something."

"It taught me how to talk dirty to yo' mama," Luis quipped.

"Whatever!" Forrest retorted. "Do me a favor."

"What you need?" Luis asked.

"Talk to your real estate friend and tell her that I want to put an offer on the last house she showed me," Forrest said.

"I'll call her today," Luis said. "Welcome back home."

XXXII

Yvette and Khalid sat in his dorm room studying for an exam; buried in books and notes up to their elbows. Khalid was stretched across his bed, and Yvette sat at his desk. Pizza boxes and soda cans littered the floor. Soft jazz played in the background.

Turiel stood still against the wall. Yvette looked at him periodically. Each time her eyes rested on him, it made her skin crawl. Why Khalid would buy such a strange statue, she could not comprehend. Every time she asked him about it, he brushed off her inquiry.

The door opened, and Belial walked in with a tall woman behind him with shoulder length, straight, black hair and baby powder white skin. She wore a tiny dress that barely reached past her hips and a shirt so low cut that the top rims of her fuchsia areolas were exposed. Cruel thin lips and fierce green eyes made her look dangerous.

Khalid sat up on his bed and took a deep breath. The woman was an eye full.

Yvette dropped her ink pen.

Belial escorted the woman to his desk and asked her to have a seat. She sat down and crossed her long legs revealing that she was not wearing underwear.

Khalid almost choked on his own spit.

"Sasha, this is my roommate, Khalid, I have been telling you about," Belial said; a mischievous grin on his face.

"Nice to meet you," she said in a thick Russian accent. "Belial has told me so much about you. You and I must talk."

Khalid could not pull his eyes from her breasts. He had never seen a woman in real life so scantily dressed. She must have been a porn star or a prostitute. She looked like one of the women in the ads in the back of free newspapers.

"Nice to meet you too," Khalid said.

Yvette cleared her throat.

"Oh yeah, this is my friend Yvette," he said trying to pull his eyes away from her peeking areolas.

"I like your friend too. We can all talk," Sasha said.

"You ain't got nothin' to say to me!" Yvette snapped. "Khalid, you betta tell this ho who she dealin' with!"

"It's not a good time," Sasha said. "Maybe I should come back later."

"No," Khalid said. "We can talk now. I know Belial would not have brought you here if what we needed to discuss wasn't important."

"You should ask your friend to leave," Belial said looking at Yvette like a speck of mold that needed to be bleached. "What you guys have to discuss is rather personal."

"We have homework to do!" Yvette barked; arms crossed and neck rolling.

Khalid turned to Yvette and kissed her on the mouth. He said, "I have to talk to Belial and his friend. I promise that we will finish this tomorrow. Okay?"

"But..." Yvette cried.

"Don't make this more than what it is. I'll talk to you later. Okay, baby," Khalid said.

He had never called her baby before. Yvette smiled through her tears.

"You promise?" she whined.

"Of course, baby," he said lifting her chin and kissing her again. "It's not what you think, so relax."

"Okay," Yvette said and gathered her belongings. He walked her to the door and kissed her slowly and deeply before he closed it behind her.

He turned to Belial.

"What's going on?" Khalid asked, walking over to his bed.

"A gift for you in honor of our deal. This is incentive for you to find me the best body that you can," Belial answered.

Sasha dropped her dressed and pushed Khalid down on the bed.

Turiel's head turned to watch what was unfolding. His wings fluttered then were still. The side of his mouth raised.

Khalid tried to sit up, but she knocked him back down with an abnormal amount of strength. He began to protest but she disrobed him quickly and sat her naked body upon him. He reached for a condom, but she grabbed his wrist and squeezed it until it dropped from his hand. Pain shot through his arm, but it was quickly forgotten when she began to grind her hips on his pelvis. Khalid moaned in ecstasy as she rode him madly. With each thrust, her spine pushed dark spikes through her skin. The spikes lined her back like shiny pebbles. Her fingernails and toenails elongated into rust colored talons. Her flickering tongue split in two as it licked up and down Khalid's neck. He cried out, but his whimpering alternated between repulsion and rhapsody.

Belial's pulse quickened. Excitement flooded through every inch of his body as he watched Khalid copulate with a demon.

XXXIII

Forrest's body hovered over Sky. His strong arms rippled beside her face as he lowered himself for a kiss. She received it gladly.

"I love you," he said before he rolled onto his side and climbed out of bed.

Sky turned onto her side to face him. She watched him walk into the bathroom. His naked body was one of the wonders of the world. Sky smiled. She answered, "I love you too!"

Sky heard the faucet turn on and the sound of Forrest's electrical toothbrush humming. He stuck his head out of the bathroom to give her a wink. Sky blushed. It was amazing how he still gave her butterflies after all the years they shared together. She listened to him shower then watched him as he toweled dry at the foot of their bed.

"Do you have to work today?" she whined. "You should stay home with me."

"I do. I wish I could," he answered while toweling his hair. "Don't you have to write today? I'm sure that your editor isn't very happy that you have missed your deadline by three months."

"He can wait," Sky grumbled. She wrapped the comforter tight around her. "I'm not getting out of bed today."

"I think you should go to the park and write," Forrest suggested. "The weather is beautiful. Besides, we won't be living in New York much longer, so you might as well suck up the city before we go."

Sky sat up in bed.

"What do you mean?" she asked; her eyes as hopeful as a child's.

"I just closed on a house in Atlanta," he said while pulling on his scrubs.

"You what?" Sky squealed gleefully. "I can't believe you bought a house without me!" She threw a pillow at him.

He dodged it easily.

"Well, if I'm going to have to live in a city that I despise, I am going to at least pick the house!" he uttered.

"Fair enough!" Sky laughed. Happy tears ran down her face. "Thank you," she mouthed.

"You're welcome, baby. I just want you to be happy," he replied.

"What neighborhood is it in?" she asked.

"South DeKalb. It's a section of Decatur. I found an unbelievable house at an amazing price. There's plenty of yard space and the people seem nice enough although they looked at me like I was singlehandedly working to gentrify their neighborhood. I think when they see you all, their fears will dissipate."

"You white people can shake up a neighborhood," Sky joked as she jumped up and did a happy dance.

"I gotta go," he said kissing her on the forehead and heading out the door.

When Sky heard the front door close, she picked up her cell phone and called Sadie.

"Hey," Sadie answered.

"How are you?" Sky asked barely able to contain her excitement.

"I'm good. How are you?" Sadie asked. "Have you begun chemo yet?"

"Nope. I think I may after I move into my new home in Atlanta!" Sky squealed.

"Atlanta?" Sadie asked; her voice as high as Sky's.

"We're coming to Atlanta. Forrest bought us a house there! He told me this morning. I don't know all the details, but I will see you soon!" Sky said.

Sadie cheered happily.

"Keep me posted. I can't wait to see you," Sadie said.

"Likewise. I love you girl!" Sky replied. "I was so worried that we may not see each other again."

"I love you too! Girl, please! I would have come up there and moved in with you and Forrest," Sadie laughed. "I knew he would come around though. He loves you too much to say no to you."

"Ain't it the truth," Sky laughed. "I kinda knew too."

"I can't wait to tell James. He is going to be so happy that ya'll are coming back," said Sadie.

"I can't wait to come back. Kiss all the kids for me. I have to go. I have a lot of things to take care of before we leave the city. Talk to you later," Sky said and hung up the phone.

She ran into the bathroom and jumped into the shower. Today was not a day for sleeping, but a day for tying up loose ends.

XXXIV

History was Khalid's least favorite subject because the facts were so bent to the agenda of the historian that most recounts of history were simply untrue; so, to him, sitting in history class was the equivalent to reading Grimm's fairytales.

Most often, history was written by the victors, the oppressors, and the dominant class of the time. Historians had the ability to spin the story anyway that made them seem superior and to justify their evils. No one wants to admit to destroying families, murdering children, enslaving nations, and brainwashing the masses with propaganda. Rarely was there an unbiased accounting of historical events that told the story of common people as well as rulers. Most often, the voices of the masses were silenced, and their true stories remained untold. Khalid knew this to be true because of the extensive knowledge of his father. The angel told him the history of humans from the very beginning. What was taught in books was only one percent of the truth; therefore, Khalid felt vindicated by sleeping peacefully as the history professor droned on.

"Wake up!" a young man yelled as he slapped Khalid on the back of the head; his big hand causing an echo to ricochet through the room.

Khalid opened his eyes and saw that the class had been dismissed. He grabbed the back of his head and looked up and saw the young man who had slapped him towering over him. There was also a trio of young men laughing in the doorway. They waved goodbye to the offending young man and left.

Khalid recognized him as one of his classmates. The honor student was wearing a purple t-shirt, purple shoes, and a purple bandana around his head. Tattoos covered his arms and the side of his face. A gang sign was tattooed on the back of his hand.

"Wake up Sleeping Beauty. Time to go," the young man said readying himself to slap Khalid again.

"Don't touch me again," Khalid said. He picked up his books and stood up. He didn't want any trouble, but he was ready just in case the young man did.

"I was trying to help you out," the young man replied, his light brown face twisted to the side and his eyes narrowed. "Nigga, don't bite the hand that feeds you."

"I appreciate you waking me up, but I'm not a nigga and don't ever touch me again," Khalid barked. "Now excuse me," Khalid said as he tried to walk around the young man.

The young man blocked Khalid's path with folded arms, a puffed-out chest, and an ego that guaranteed disaster.

"Whatchu gone do?" the young man asked.

"I'm going to leave, and you are going to move," Khalid answered; his eyes narrowing and his shoulders rounding forward.

"Who gone make me?" the young man laughed.

"Dude, move," Khalid said.

He sidestepped the young man, but the young man blocked Khalid's path again.

"You gone make things real hard for yourself," Khalid warned. "I don't want no trouble. Stop playing with me."

"Young blood, obviously you don't know who you talking to. Say please and I might let you leave," the young man said.

He stepped into Khalid's face; his forehead almost touching Khalid's.

"I know exactly who I'm talking to. You are Duane Smith a.k.a. Lil Smooky, a twenty-year-old hood booger from Nashville, TN who thinks he's bad because he joined a gang and spent a year in juvenile detention. You have a high IQ but the common sense of a pine needle. You pretend to be a player to disguise your homosexual yearnings, and you are harassing me because you think, because I am young, that I am someone you could punk, but you are sadly mistaken. You have two seconds to get out of my face before I beat yo' ass like your jailbird daddy used to. Obviously, you don't know who I am," Khalid hissed; his spit sprinkling Duane's face.

Duane stepped back and punched Khalid in the face so hard that Khalid's head snapped back then forward. He thought he would blackout, but quickly regained his footing. Adrenaline rushed through Khalid's veins like a hot river of energy. He laughed aloud.

Duane swung again but missed. Khalid stepped under Duane's punch and hit him with two uppercuts. The educated gangster hit the floor. Khalid pounced on top of him and wrapped his hands around his neck.

"Say you sorry," Khalid hissed.

Duane coughed and shook his head *no*.

Khalid squeezed tighter. Gurgling sounds faded into silence. Duane's eyes went blank.

"See what you made me do!" Khalid yelled. His voice echoed through the wall like thunder.

Khalid stood up and kicked the dead body. He pulled his cell phone out of his pocket and texted Belial. Within minutes, Belial was in the empty classroom with Khalid and the dead man.

"Here's your body," Khalid said; rubbing the side of his face. His cheekbone was beginning to swell. Duane packed a mean punch.

Belial walked over to the dead man and stooped over him. He examined the body from head to toe, then turned to Khalid.

"I don't want that body," Belial said; a frown on his flaking face.

"Why not?" Khalid asked. "He's young, strong, and healthy."

"He's marked up like a coloring book," Belial retorted. "I want someone who doesn't look like a walking stereotype!"

Khalid rubbed his face. He opened his mouth to stretch his jawbone. It hurt. He kicked the dead man again.

"Well, you should have been more specific!" Khalid barked.

"You should have been more selective," Belial barked back.

Khalid rubbed the side of his face again. He hoped that it didn't swell too much. He didn't want to look like he had been in an altercation.

"We need to get out of here before someone sees us," said Khalid.

"What are you going to do with the body?" Belial asked.

"Leave it. Not my problem," Khalid answered picking up his belongings and walking out of the classroom before Belial could say another word.

XXXV

The boy's locker room in Uriel's high school was full of sweaty jocks getting in and out of the showers. Steam floated through the room as laughter and cheers bounced off the concrete walls. The team was celebrating their victorious game from earlier that night. It was a good game against a long-time rival that went into overtime. In the end, Uriel's team had pulled off the win.

Uriel gave one of his teammates a high five and threw a towel over his shoulder as he headed to the showers. He liked to wait until all the other boys were done before he showered because he did not like being naked in a room full of people; especially a room full of funky boys. He felt that boys played too much. They were always popping each other with towels, trying to wrestle, comparing penis sizes, or doing something else completely ridiculous. Uriel had no desire to engage in any of those activities while clothed, so he definitely didn't want to entertain it while naked.

He made his way to an empty shower near the back of the locker room, far away from his other teammates. Uriel turned on the shower and let the tepid water run through his thick hair, down his face onto the rest of his body. He soaped up briskly, toweled off, and dressed quickly before he walked back into the central area of the locker room. His teammates were gone.

Uriel looked at the time on his cell phone. He couldn't believe he had been in the shower for a quarter hour. That was unusual for him since he usually finished in less than five minutes. It was even more unusual that the locker room had cleared out so quickly and completely.

The locker room was eerily empty. He couldn't believe that he hadn't noticed the sudden quiet while he was showering. After all, the locker room's volume was always deafening. The current silence unnerved Uriel. He packed up his belongings as fast as he could and slung his bag over his shoulder. He slammed his locker shut and locked the lock.

A warm hand touched Uriel's shoulder. He spun around. There was no one there. He turned back towards the door and Mrs. Covington was standing in front of him.

Uriel stepped backward.

"Grandma?" Uriel uttered nervously. He blinked his eyes twice and looked around him to make sure he was seeing what he was seeing.

"Yes sweetheart," Mrs. Covington answered with a tinge of sadness in her voice.

"Why are you here?" he asked.

He was not afraid by her other visits, mainly because he was coming out of or going into a sleep state, but it was something about being wide awake in the empty locker room and seeing the distressed look on her face that alarmed him.

"Your brother is in danger. Only you can help him," she said; one of her eyes becoming strangely transparent. "His father is back, but he is not the danger. Turiel is in danger too."

Uriel was confused. How could the angel be back after he was banished, and how could he and Khalid both be in danger?

"Khalid has befriended a worthless thing!" Mrs. Covington squawked as if she was in pain.

Uriel swallowed hard. He searched her face. It looked different; the way her nose curved, and her lips were shaped. He wanted to reach out and touch her but something inside of him warned him not to.

"Grandma," he whispered.

"Help him," her voice wavered.

Half of her face faded into the background of the locker room. A look of fear stretched her remaining eye. The bottom half of her body was gone. The upper half of her torso was threatening to dwindle also.

"Help…" her entire mouth faded leaving only the top quarter of her face; her perfectly arched brow accenting her melancholy eye. Her lone eye blinked, then was gone.

"Grandma!" Uriel cried out.

He heard no answer. He knew in his heart that he would never see her again.

XXXVI

Sky squealed when the car pulled into the driveway of their new home. She clapped like a three-year-old and tapped her feet on the car floor. An open-mouthed smile broadened her face.

It was a three-story house with a full basement. Colorful flowers lined the walkway. Wind chimes sang from every corner of the porch. A large flowering tree sat in the middle of the yard. A cast iron table with matching chairs sat under it. The front door was painted a vivid purple.

Forrest pulled a remote from the dashboard and opened one of the doors of the two-car garage.

"This place is beautiful," Earth cooed.

The other children nodded in agreement.

"Daddy! You did good!" Venus chimed. "I can't wait to see inside."

Proudly, Jupiter embraced Forrest's shoulder from the back seat.

Mars ignored the house. He was more enchanted by the huge front yard and the giant tree out front that he planned on climbing as soon as he got a chance.

The car came to a halt and the children raced into the house. They filed up the stairs calling dibs on bedrooms. All four marked their territory by throwing their bags in the room that they wanted. Sky and Forrest walked into the master bedroom on the main floor and sighed in awe of the large space.

"You did so good," Sky complimented as she walked into the spacious walk-in closet.

Forrest smiled.

"I really love this house," Sky admitted. "I could not have picked better myself."

"I knew you would," Forrest said. "I know you like the back of my hand. When I saw this place, I knew you would squeal like a pig."

Sky laughed.

"You are so right!" she agreed. "I really love this place.

"I can't wait to turn half of the basement into a game room. You can do whatever you want with the other half."

"Got everything all planned out, huh?" Sky smirked.

"Yep," Forrest agreed.

He walked over to a window and looked out into the backyard. He said, "I think we should put up a swing set for Mars and maybe a gazebo for you. Do you like the front porch?"

"It's lovely," she answered.

"And the wind chimes?" he asked.

"Music to my ears," she said.

"I knew you would like it. It's kinda romantic. I can see us on the porch drinking lemonade and playing with our great grandchildren in the future," Forrest said still staring out of the window.

Sky began to cry.

Forrest turned away from the window and rushed to her. He put his arms around her and apologized. It was not his intention to cause her pain. It was stupid of him to dream about a future that they may never have together. There was nothing that he could say that could remove his foot from his mouth. It was lodged too far down his throat.

"How far does Sadie live from us?" Sky asked into his chest; her hot breath and tears clinging to his shirt and warming her face. She instantly forgave him because she knew that to have a successful marriage, one must have a fleeting memory. Besides, it was foolish to be angry about someone for waxing optimistic about the future, even a future that was bleak.

"About fifteen minutes," he answered.

"Cool. We should go visit after we settle in. What time will the movers arrive?" she asked; wiping her eyes.

"Tomorrow after two," he answered.

"Looks like tonight is a sleeping bag night," Sky replied; letting Forrest go and walking out of the bedroom. It was time for her to explore her dream house.

XXXVII

Police officers swarmed the college campus. Flashing blue lights threw designs on Khalid's walls as he looked down from his dorm room window. The EMT workers rolled Duane's sheet covered body out of the history department building into the back of an ambulance. Yvette stared out of the window with Khalid. Belial lounged on his bed reading a dusty old book.

"I wonder what happened?" Yvette questioned. "Duane was a cool dude. Who would kill him?"

"He was a jerk," Khalid responded nonchalantly as he walked away from the window and plopped down on his bed. He and Belial exchanged quick glances.

"How can you say that? A boy is dead!" she exclaimed. "Sometimes you can be so cold hearted!"

Khalid looked at her and said nothing.

There was a knock on the door.

"Answer that," Khalid told Yvette.

She furiously spun around, her braids swinging like golden cords, and headed to the door. It was frustrating when Khalid didn't respond to her. Sometimes she wished that she was brave enough to slap him across the face and dump him, but she loved him too much and felt like he was the best thing that ever happened to her despite his occasional cruelty.

She opened the door. A middle-aged police officer stood in the doorway with an annoyed expression on her face. A younger male officer stood next to her.

"Is Khalid Tucker here?" the female officer asked Yvette.

Yvette stepped to the side and pointed to Khalid. Khalid stood up and walked over to the officers.

"I am Khalid Tucker. How can I help you?" he asked.

"I am Officer Hernandez, and this is my partner Officer Gordon. We would like to ask you a few questions," she said.

"Sure," responded Khalid.

"Mr. Tucker, did you know Duane Smith?" she asked as she scribbled something on a notepad.

Belial looked up from his book curiously.

"I knew of him," Khalid answered. "He was in my history class."

"He was murdered earlier today, and you were the last one that was seen with him," she said as she stared deeply into his eyes as if she was looking for a visual confession of guilt.

Yvette gasped.

The officer took note.

"I'm sorry to hear that," Khalid responded. "Last I saw him, he slapped me in the back of my head to wake me up after class."

"You didn't like that; did you Mr. Tucker?" she asked, folding her arms in front of her, her olive face showing her suspicion of him.

"I did not," Khalid confessed, folding his arms in front of him. "Do you like getting hit?"

Officer Hernandez scribbled something on her pad and asked, "What did you do after he slapped you?"

"I picked up my things and left," he answered.

"A big guy like you allowed a scrawny little guy like Duane to slap you and you did nothing?" Officer Hernandez chuckled. Her partner laughed with her.

"Duane was a notorious gang member. I had no desire to get into it with him," Khalid answered. "I am a college freshman and four years younger than he is. He knows more people than I do."

"Word around campus is that you are the popular one," the lady cop responded.

Khalid grabbed Yvette around her waist and pulled her toward him. He said, "I'm a lover not a fighter."

Yvette blushed.

"Really?" Officer Hernandez asked. "What happened to your cheek? It looks a little bruised."

"Me and my girl like it rough sometimes," Khalid remarked. He winked at the officer and flashed a charming smile.

"Loverboy, you need to come downtown with us," the female officer said while pulling her cuffs from her belt.

"I don't think so," Khalid responded. He looked into her eyes and the woman dropped the handcuffs on the floor. A shiver ran down her spine and a tear ran from her left eye. She stumbled backward into her partner. He grabbed her by the arm to steady her balance.

"Are you okay?" he asked her.

She nodded slowly, not taking her eyes off Khalid.

Khalid said, "You have no evidence against me and no right to arrest me. I know my rights. I suggest that you and Officer Friendly over there go back to the precinct and leave me alone. Do we understand each other?"

"Yes," Officer Hernandez answered; her eyes glazed over and her voice monotone. Pressure filled her chest. She found it hard to breathe.

"Are you okay?" Officer Gordon asked her again.

Officer Hernandez nodded.

"We're sorry to have bothered you," she droned and grabbed her partner's arm and pulled him down the hall behind her. The two officers turned the corner and were gone.

"What did you do to her?" Yvette asked; confused about the officer's sudden compliance to Khalid's wishes.

"I just have a way with women." Khalid smiled and kissed Yvette on the mouth. He jumped back on his bed.

"Why didn't you tell me that you were the last one with Duane?" Yvette asked suspiciously. She was always aware that there was something dangerous behind Khalid's eyes, but she was unsure if he was capable of murder. One thing she was sure of was that no one was going to hit Khalid and get away with it. People who interacted with Khalid had an unexplainable fear and respect for him.

"There was nothing to tell," Khalid said. He picked up a book and began to read. "Let it go or let yourself out."

Yvette picked up a book and uncomfortably sat on the bed next to him. For the first time in their relationship, Yvette felt afraid.

XXXVⅠⅠⅠ

"How do you like school?" Uriel asked Earth as he tossed a football to Mars. Venus and Jupiter sat on James's and Sadie's back porch scrolling through their cell phones, oblivious to everyone around them.

"It's cool I guess. My classes were easy to find, and people are nice so far. I'm glad that you're there. It makes it easier to get acclimated," Earth answered.

She sat cross-legged on the ground. The thick grass felt good against her skin. A sharp fall wind blew past her threatening to steal away her late summer comfort.

"I'm glad we have two classes together. It makes me seem cool to already know the new girl," Uriel laughed as he ran backward to catch the ball. "Maybe you should join some activities. It makes school a lot more fun."

"Maybe," Earth mumbled as she ran her fingers through blades of grass. She plucked a clover and stuck it behind her ear.

"Wanna go for a walk?" Uriel asked as he threw the ball back to Mars. "I'm kinda tired of playing catch."

Mars pouted.

"I promise we'll play again after we get back," Uriel said to Mars.

Mars smiled and nodded okay.

"Sure," Earth answered, getting up from the grass. She put her sandals on and followed Uriel out of the back gate.

The street was long and quiet. Trees lined the sidewalks and bright flowers decorated every green space.

The houses were all painted a different bright color. Each mailbox looked like a folk-art piece.

"Your neighborhood is so peaceful," Earth commented as she enjoyed the singing birds perched on the powerlines above. She hummed a little as they tweeted.

"Yes, it is. I like it a lot," Uriel responded. "I take walks to think clearly."

The two walked to a small lake surrounded by benches. Earth sat down in the grass. Uriel started skipping rocks on the water.

"Did you want to move to Atlanta?" Uriel asked as he threw a small stone.

"Yes. I hated school in New York. The only person I will miss there is my friend Simone. Other than that, good riddance," Earth answered.

"Why did you hate school? I love school," Uriel asked.

He stopped throwing stones and sat directly in front of Earth. He liked to look people in their eyes when he spoke to them. Eyes told secrets that mouths tried to hide. Eye contact made conversations much more intimate and interesting.

"I was picked on a lot," Earth admitted. "I don't know why. I didn't bother anyone."

"People are stupid sometimes. I'm sure that they were just jealous because you're so beautiful," Uriel responded sincerely.

Earth blushed. She said, "You must be talking about my sister. She's the beautiful one."

"She's cute, but I think you're beautiful," Uriel said averting his eyes. Suddenly, he felt uncomfortable.

"Thank you," Earth whispered.

"You're welcome," Uriel said, getting back up to pick up stones.

A long silence stood between them until Earth disrupted the quiet.

"I'm glad to be here because of Mama. Before she dies, she wanted to be near Auntie. Sadie," Earth said full of hopelessness.

Uriel dropped the stone and sat beside her. He placed his arm around her shoulder and squeezed. Earth began to cry.

"Please don't cry," Uriel said. "Your mother will be okay."

"I don't think so," she cried. "I overheard her on the phone telling someone that she had stage four cancer and that it was so widespread that there was little to do to help it."

"She will be okay," Uriel said. "God will heal her. I know it," he promised. "All you have to do is believe."

"I don't know if I can," Earth wept.

"Do you consider me a friend?" he asked.

"Of course, I do," she answered through sobs. "You've become my best friend."

"Well, believe that I would never lie to you. Your mother will be okay," he said with authority.

Earth looked up into his eyes. She wanted desperately to have the faith that he did, but she did not.

She did not have an ounce of it. She allowed her head to drop onto his shoulder.

Uriel kissed her on the forehead and rubbed her arm as he held her tight.

Earth smiled through her tears. Maybe it was something that he knew that she did not. She found peace in that.

XXX|X

The college campus was abuzz with students. Some were smiling from ear to ear. Some were cussing like sailors. Khalid and Yvette walked across campus hand in hand talking about arbitrary things. They felt good about the exams that they had taken earlier that day and had decided to celebrate by going to lunch at the local diner about five blocks from campus.

As they walked down the busy street, a couple of unmarked black cars drove past the couple and stopped a few yards away. Khalid noticed a police car in his peripheral. It parked a block away, and then another one pulled up in front of Khalid.

Yvette grabbed Khalid's arm tightly. Her heart pounded so hard that Khalid could feel her pulse through her wrists on his arm.

"Are you Khalid Tucker," a fat pink officer asked with a deep southern accent. He chewed a toothpick and stood with his thumbs in his belt.

Two officers exited the police car parked behind the fat pink officer's car and four officers emerged from the unmarked black cars.

"I am," Khalid answered. He pulled Yvette behind him to shield her from harm. "How can I help you?"

"I need you to come with me," the pink officer said, the toothpick in his mouth moving around like a conductor's stick.

"Why do I need to come with you?" Khalid asked. "I'm a college student. I'm not involved with any illegal activity. I'm a minor. I think you may need to talk to my parents."

Khalid turned and tried to walk away, but the fat pink cop grabbed his arm and squeezed.

"You don't move until I tell you to move," the officer said, the toothpick getting softer and wetter.

Khalid snatched away from the officer.

"Don't put your filthy hands on me!" Khalid growled.

"Go with them Khalid," Yvette urged. She clung to him like a sloth to a tree. "I don't want you to get hurt. You know how cops love to kill black boys," she whined.

"Boy, you better listen to your gal," the pink officer said; placing his hand on the handle of his gun. His words were like a long drawn out song. Khalid half expected someone to start whistling Dixie.

The other officers placed their hands on their weapons.

"Why are you harassing me?" Khalid asked. "Are you arresting me for something?"

"You're suspected of murder son. If you come with me, I won't need to arrest you. We just have a few questions to ask you," the fat pink officer answered. He removed his hand from his gun handle and reached for his cuffs instead.

"I haven't done anything to anyone! You haven't read me my rights and I request to speak with my lawyer," Khalid hissed. "If you have no evidence against me, I suggest you move out of my way!"

The officer's round pink face bent downward with displeasure. Backtalk from ornery teenagers made him very unhappy. A matter of fact, it downright pissed him off. He grabbed Khalid by the shirt and slammed him to the ground.

Yvette let out an ear-piercing scream. Nearby students ran towards them with their cell phones on record.

"You have the right to remain silent," the police officer said as he kicked Khalid in the ribs. "Anything you say can be used against you in a court of law!" the cop spit his toothpick on Khalid's chest. "You have the right to have an attorney present," he said before another officer joined in with a punch to Khalid's face.

"If you can't afford an attorney, one will be appointed to you," the fat pink cop hollered as he pulled Khalid up from the ground and slammed him into the side of the police car.

"You ready to comply, boy?" the pink officer asked.

Khalid turned to face him and spit in the pink officer's eyes.

Wrathfully, the pink officer took his stick and struck Khalid across the face with it. Dizziness rocked Khalid as he fell back against the police car.

Yvette pulled out her cell phone to record the battery, but another officer knocked it out of her hand cracking the screen. He then pushed her so hard that she fell onto the grass. She jumped up and ran away screaming.

A large crowd of college students gathered around Khalid and the attacking officers. Panic and anger filled them as they witnessed their Student Council President being abused by the police.

Students began to scream, "Let him go!" as they picked up stones and began to throw them at the police officers. One of the officers pulled his gun and pointed it at the crowd.

"Back up," the officer screamed, his brown face dripping with sweat.

The students dropped their rocks and stepped backward but continued to demand Khalid's release.

"Leave him alone!" a girl screamed as she pushed her way through the crowd.

Khalid looked up; a weak smile on his blood caked face. It was Venus. He had forgotten that she was coming to visit.

She made her way to Khalid until she was face to face with three police officers.

"Do not disrupt police business!" a skinny white officer yelled. The female officer tapped the handle of her gun.

"You have no right to hurt him! He did nothing wrong!" Venus barked refusing to lose ground.

"You are going to force me to arrest you," the skinny officer threatened as she neared Venus.

"You just gone have to arrest me then!" Venus snapped. "Because I'm not going anywhere! What you are doing is illegal and there is a crap load of witnesses here to attest to it! Let him go!"

The skinny officer forced Venus to the ground and snapped handcuffs around her wrists.

Hot anger raged through Khalid. His eyes blacked out. He grabbed the pink officer by the neck and threw him into the officers behind him. They fell down like bowling pins.

Khalid whispered, "Die!" and each officer that looked into his eyes grabbed their chest and screamed out. Each felt like their heart was being squeezed by an invisible fist. Suddenly, their screams went dead like their bodies.

Khalid ran over to Venus and unlocked her cuffs. He helped her up from the ground and hugged her tight.

"Are you okay," he asked after brushing the grass from her clothes.

Venus nodded.

Filled with anguish and excitement, he hugged her again.

"Thank you for sticking up for me," Khalid said into her ear. The softness of her skin and the sweet smell of her hair, vanilla and lilac, made it difficult for him to let her go.

Yvette came running back through the crowd towards Khalid and Venus.

"Are you okay, baby?" she asked while touching the part of his face that was not nestled into the side of Venus's neck.

"I was so worried about you! I'm so glad you okay!" Yvette cried.

Venus broke Khalid's embrace and stepped back.

"You weren't worried about me! You left me here to get beaten and locked up," Khalid spat between his teeth.

"Baby, what was I supposed to do?" Yvette cried. "I told you not to give them trouble!"

"You were supposed to have his back," Venus snapped.

Yvette cut her eyes at Venus. She balled her fists.

Venus laughed.

"Don't come for me unless I send for you! Trust, you don't want no part of me," Venus huffed.

The fearlessness in Venus's eyes matched the darkness of Khalid's. Discernment told Yvette that it would not be wise to pick a fight with Venus.

"Baby," Yvette whined; grabbing the sides of Khalid's face and trying to kiss him.

"Don't call me baby," Khalid hissed, and pushed her away. "Don't call me period!" he spat.

Khalid grabbed Venus's hand and exited the crowd before the flashing blue lights a block away arrived to collect their dead brethren.

Yvette stood, with mouth stretched wide, among the awe-struck students watching Khalid and Venus fade behind the campus buildings.

XL

"How are you feeling?" Sadie asked while sponging Sky's leathery forehead. The chemotherapy and radiation worked diligently to steal Sky's beauty. The beauty heist was almost a success, but the radiance of Sky's determination to live for her family helped to retain her true essence.

Sky's ashy complexion made her slim face look like a skull. Her beautiful red hair was now a thin ball of fluff that stuck out like strands of wire every time her head lifted from the pillow. Dark burgundy skin circled her green eyes giving her the appearance of a battered wife.

"Want some more ice?" Sadie asked.

Sky nodded.

Sadie handed Sky a cup of crushed ice from the nightstand.

Sky ate it greedily.

"You didn't answer my question," Sadie said, climbing in the bed next to Sky. Sadie lifted her arm, so Sky could use it as a pillow.

"How do I look like I feel?" Sky retorted. "I'm too sick for you to be askin' me stupid questions."

"I ask you what I want," Sadie snapped back. "I need to know if you need more pain medicine. Is your skin still burning?"

"My skin is always burnin'," Sky griped.

"What do you want me to do?" Sadie asked.

"Find a cure for cancer," Sky whispered.

"If I could, I would," Sadie replied; yawning big and wide like a lion.

"Go home and have sex with your husband! At least one of us should be having fun," Sky said; a crooked smile on her face. "You're spending too much time here."

"I'm taking care of you," Sadie responded fluffing Sky's pillows.

"I'm as good as I'm gonna get. You need to take care of yo' man," Sky replied. "Things were getting better with you too."

"I know," Sadie sighed. "I just want to be here for you."

"I know," Sky replied. She held Sadie's hands in hers and continued, "but you have to be balanced. He needs you too."

"Don't worry about us. We will be okay," Sadie snapped feeling a little rueful about being away from home so much. She was tired of feeling guilty all the time. If she spent too much time with James she felt that she was neglecting Sky. If she spent too much time with Sky, she felt like she was neglecting James. Uriel was the only one who seemed to understand that she was being pulled in all directions like drum skin.

Sky touched Sadie's crestfallen face.

"You need to stop pouting. I'm the sick one!" Sky joked.

Sadie stuck her lip out further.

"But, since you can't stop being so extra, can you do me a favor?" Sky asked.

"Anything," Sadie answered laying her head on the top of Sky's.

"When I die, will you help Forrest raise my children? They are too much for him to handle alone," Sky asked.

"Don't talk like that! You're going to beat this thing!" Sadie scolded. "You are going to raise your own children!"

"No, I'm not," Sky whispered. "I saw my mama yesterday. She was sitting at the foot of my bed; waiting to take me over yonder."

Sadie laughed with tears in her eyes. She replied, "You are so dramatic; such a writer! When was the last time anyone said over yonder?"

Sky smiled.

"I'm serious though. I saw her for the first time since she died. Sadie, she was just sittin' there staring at me with a smirk on her face; wearin' yellow like she had just finished prayin' to Oshun. She had flowers in her hair and smelled like honey," said Sky.

"It was just a dream," Sadie said. "You ain't going anywhere anytime soon. Like I said, you will beat the hell out of cancer!"

"Just in case I don't," Sky whispered, her emerald eyes glossing over. "Promise me that you will help take care of my children."

"I promise," Sadie promised. She wrapped her arms around Sky and challenged God, unsure if he or she existed, to heal Sky.

XLI

The school bell rang, and the students scattered like baby spiders being squeezed from a giant egg. They tossed books in lockers, ran down the hallways, kissed lovers, wrestled, and disappeared through the front doors.

Uriel waited patiently for Earth to emerge from the girl's bathroom. It seemed like she was taking forever. After what seemed like an eternity, she emerged with a fresh coat of lip gloss on.

"Hey," Earth greeted, surprised and slightly embarrassed to see him. She thought that he would have left after she had spent fifteen minutes in the bathroom. Her stomach was giving her trouble, but it was all better now.

"Hey," Uriel answered. "Want me to get that?"

"What?" Earth asked.

"Your books," he responded; a crooked smile on his face.

"Sure," Earth said as she handed her backpack over.

Uriel's kindness reminded her of one of the amorous characters her mother wrote about in her books. Uriel was kind of romantic like her father Forrest. The thought made Earth's belly tingle.

"Want to go to my house? My mom is probably with your mom and my dad is always at work since ya'll moved back to Atlanta," said Uriel as they walked out of the school yard onto the sidewalk.

Earth felt nervous. She had never been home alone with a boy that wasn't one of her brothers.

Uriel sensed her unease and said, "We can play video games and I can make you a sandwich. If you don't feel comfortable, we can sit on the porch."

"Okay," Earth agreed. The porch sounded like a less intense place to be.

They walked along in silence until they turned onto the next street.

"Can I tell you something?" Uriel asked.

"Yeah," she answered. "You can tell me anything. You're the only friend I have."

"Please don't think I'm crazy, but I have to tell someone, or I will go crazy!" he said.

"You can tell me anything. I would never think you are crazy," Earth replied as she strolled behind Uriel.

They arrived at his street. His house was the third one on the right. He climbed the stairs three at a time.

Earth stood at the bottom trying to decide if she wanted to stay outside or go inside the house.

He unlocked the door and opened it. He looked at Earth still standing at the bottom of the stairs and said, "I'll run in to get us something to drink and to put these books down. You can sit on the porch or in the grass. Whatever makes you comfortable."

Uriel went inside and came back out moments later with two glasses of strawberry lemonade and a bag of chips.

Earth was sitting on the grass under a tree, barefoot and cross-legged. She reached out to receive her glass and took a large swallow sucking a piece of ice into her mouth. She chewed it slowly as she waited for Uriel to take off his shoes and sit down next to her.

"Nothing feels better than the earth beneath your feet," Earth sighed.

"Of course, you think so," laughed Uriel. He laid back and watched the clouds. "That one looks like a rabbit with a cell phone in its paw," he said.

Earth laid back and quickly spotted the cloud. It did look like a rabbit holding a cell phone.

"What did you have to tell me?" she asked unable to tear her eyes away from the rabbit cloud.

"I have been seeing my dead grandma," Uriel said, holding his breath; almost waiting for Earth to laugh at him.

"Me too," she responded still looking at the cloud.

Uriel turned to her and asked, "What do you mean?" He wondered what would be the odds of Venus seeing Mrs. Covington too.

"I have been seeing my grandmother around my mom. That's why I know that my mom is going to die," Earth answered. "The dead always come to visit the dying."

"If that were true, that means that you and I are dying because we are the ones who are seeing dead people," said Uriel.

"Well, if you put it that way," Earth retorted.

She took another sip of lemonade and grabbed a hand full of chips. She ate most of them and tossed the other half onto the grass.

"Don't waste food," Uriel scolded.

"What's with you and food? I notice that you always make sure you clean your plate and cringe every time someone throws food away?" Earth asked crunching the chips into a powder and mixing it with dirt.

"My dad taught us to never waste food. When he was young, he knew how it felt to be hungry. When he became a man, he made sure that we always had enough to eat and twice a month my dad, brother, and I make lunches for about two hundred kids in his old neighborhood," Uriel shared.

"Wow, your dad is pretty awesome," Earth said feeling guilty about tossing the chips.

"Yep, James Tucker rocks!" Uriel exclaimed. "He's the best man I know."

Earth sighed quietly and searched for another image in the clouds.

"Your mother isn't going to die," Uriel said. "Stop saying that. You can speak things into existence. There is power in words."

Earth shook her head. There was no need to argue about her mother's mortality. Changing the subject, she asked, "Where have you been seeing yours?"

"Different places. She came to me in my room, my dad's car, and the last time in the locker room at school," replied Uriel. "The last time she came, it kind of scared me."

"What happened?" Earth asked.

She turned on her side to face him. He turned on his side to face her. They were face to face with only a few blades of grass between them.

"She was telling me to see about Khalid and she started to fade. It was like she was being erased," he said.

"Erased?" she asked, a bit confused.

"Yeah, her body parts started to fade piece by piece. At one point, only her eye was left. A strange feeling came over me as I watched her fade away," he said.

"What was it?" Earth asked.

"I knew I would never see her again," he answered sadly. "Something about her leaving like that made me think that she was feeling some kind of pain. Do you think my grandmother went to Hell?"

"Of course not!" Earth countered. "God would not have used you to free her from her suffering just to put her in an eternity of suffering."

Uriel dropped his eyes.

Earth moved closer to him and rested her hand on the side of his face. Her hand was warm and covered in grains of salt from the chips she had eaten.

"If she were in Hell, why would she come to visit you? Seems like to me, she would be too busy running from the devil!" Earth responded.

Uriel looked up into her eyes and laughed aloud. She laughed along with him. They laughed so hard that they found their faces almost touching. The laughter stopped.

Uriel leaned in and kissed Earth gently on the lips. His feet felt hot. The heat suddenly rushed up his legs. He pulled back quickly as if he was stung by a bee; a sweet bee so full of honey that it might just explode.

"I'm so sorry. We better get you home," he said as he jumped up and ran into the house to get her books.

Earth's face turned into a ripe strawberry. Her stomach tingled like it never had before.

XLII

Khalid flashed a tall, rough looking security guard a fake ID. The big man twisted his lips to the side and huffed. It was obvious that Khalid was not thirty years old. Khalid grudgingly handed the guard a hundred-dollar bill, the very last of his money for the semester, and the big man moved to the side and allowed Khalid to enter.

Smoke filled the bar in clouds of smelly gray. Loud music pulsated from old speakers that thumped from the corners of the room. On a round stage, in the middle of the room, two topless women slid down metal poles. They looked a little older than Khalid imagined they would be. They were still kinda pretty he guessed, but he estimated their ages to be in the early fifties or maybe late forties. Khalid figured that maybe he was in a place where strippers went to die.

Khalid made his way to an empty table near the back of the room. A woman wearing a leotard with fishnet stockings, a metallic orange wig, and earrings with missing stones asked him if he wanted a drink. He shook his head, declining the offer. She rolled her big hazel eyes and walked away.

Khalid scanned the room until they landed on a middle-aged Hispanic male with a palm full of cash throwing money at the dancing women on the stage. The man had a strong build, a pleasant face, and was of average height. There was nothing eye catching about him in a positive or negative way. Khalid watched as the man drank glass after glass of alcohol. After his money ran out, he stumbled out of the back door of the strip club. Khalid followed behind him.

"Excuse me," Khalid asked the drunken man.

The staggering man turned around and looked at Khalid.

"What?" the man slurred. He stumbled as if he was doing the mumbo to music only he could hear.

"What time is it?" Khalid asked; the shadow of the building hiding half his face.

"Do I look like Father Time to you!" the drunken man belched. "Get away from me you little twerp!"

"I think you are too drunk to drive sir," Khalid said.

"Mind your business!" the drunkard yelped.

He pulled his keys out of his pocket and tried to unlock his car to no avail. He was too drunk to push the button on the key fob or to put the key in the key hole.

"Let me help you," Khalid said as he walked over to the man.

The man swung his arm to ward off Khalid, but Khalid dodged it. Khalid stepped back and looked at the man who seemed to sober up enough to take notice of Khalid's blacked-out eyes staring back at him.

The man grabbed his chest and stumbled backward as a pain mounted in his chest, but it left as quickly as it came.

Khalid changed his mind. Willing the man to die was too easy. Khalid wanted to feel the warmth from the man's body chill slowly into lifelessness, so he snatched the keys out of the drunken man's hand and stabbed him in the neck with them until a thick fountain of blood rushed from his neck coating Khalid's hand like a liquid glove. Khalid stabbed and stabbed the man until his arms stopped flailing. He hit the ground; a lump of mutilated flesh.

Khalid hoisted the dead man up over his shoulder and took him to his car. After wrapping the man's neck with some rags, he found in the trunk, Khalid put the man into the car and drove back to campus. He parked the car and carried him up the back stairs to his dorm room. Unable to pull his key from his pocket because he was holding the dead man, Khalid kicked the door lightly with his foot hoping that no one would hear him in the hallway in the middle of the night.

Belial opened the door and Khalid pushed through quickly, dropping the man on the floor. Khalid went into the bathroom to gather cleaning supplies and to put on gloves, and then rushed back into the hallway and down the stairs to ensure that no blood was left behind. He went to the car and cleaned his fingerprints off of everything. He then drove the car across town, threw the supplies in his backpack, and caught the bus back to his college.

Two hours later, Khalid walked back into his dorm room. Belial sat on the corner of his bed reading as usual. Khalid was surprised to see that he still was wearing the same decaying body that he had been wearing since Khalid had known him. The dead man was still lying in the middle of the floor.

"What's going on?" Khalid asked, angry that the dead man had not been possessed by Belial.

"What do you mean?" Belial asked not looking up from his book.

"I brought you a healthy body. Why aren't you wearing it?" Khalid asked, breathing hard from the night's labor. He removed his bloody shirt, put it in a plastic bag, and went to the refrigerator. He emptied old food, sauces, and liquids into the bag, onto the soiled shirt, then tossed it all into the trash.

"I don't want him," Belial replied flippantly.

"What's wrong with him?" Khalid roared.

Anger raged in him so great that his blackening eyes extended to his forehead and cheekbones as if he was wearing a shadowy mask.

"Keep your voice down. It's not wise to bring attention to our room," Belial said as he flipped a page.

Turiel stared from the corner of the room, his eyes indignant. A wrinkle ran across his forehead as his golden brows furrowed.

"You've upset your daddy," Belial laughed not looking up. "I can feel his energy shift."

Khalid looked at the angel noticing the change in his face.

"What's wrong with this guy?" a distressed Khalid asked, sounding like the sixteen-year-old that he was.

"Too old," Belial answered. "Too old and his liver is probably shot, not to mention the hack job you did on his neck. Was I supposed to walk around like a victim of a shark attack?"

Khalid dropped down on his bed and buried his face in his hands. He wanted to cry but could not. He took a deep breath and looked up.

"Please don't make me drag this body back out of this room," Khalid said.

Belial put the book down, his shadow still sitting on the bed, and went to his desk to open the ancient box. Belial said something in a foreign language and the lid flew open. Thousands upon thousands of light beings swarmed around the dead body and consumed it in a matter of seconds. Belial spoke again, and the creatures returned to the box. Nothing was left of the dead man but a skeleton wearing clothes.

"Dispose of the remains. Next time I won't be so benevolent if you bring me back a subpar body," Belial said as he picked his book up and began to read again.

Khalid gathered the bones and clothes into his backpack and exited the room. Fear and frustration filled him. There was no pleasing that demon.

XL|||

Forrest drove down the busy interstate, as slow as a snail, fighting the impulse to lay on his horn until his car battery died. It had been a long day. He had worked in the emergency room doing lifesaving surgeries all day. All he wanted was to get in his bed and go to sleep, but Atlanta traffic was as horrendous as usual. It would not allow him to get to the bed he longed for, the bed that he had been fantasizing about all day long between cutting and sewing maimed bodies. He grumbled under his breath as he switched radio stations. Slowly but surely, he made it off the exit and drove nearly five miles to his house. He turned into his driveway and sluggishly climbed out of his car and forced one foot in front of the other until he reached his front door. Forrest opened his front door.

"Daddy!" Mars screamed running full speed to his father and jumping into his arms.

Forrest stumbled backward but was able to prevent himself from falling. He allowed himself to smile.

"Hello son!" Forrest said as he kissed his son on the cheek and put him back on the floor. "I missed you buddy."

"I missed you too Daddy. How was work today?" Mars asked.

"Very busy," Forrest replied. "I am beyond tired."

"Did you see some guts?" Mars asked with his eyes stretched wide.

"I saw lots of guts," Forrest answered truthfully. He had seen more guts than he had seen in a very long time. It seemed that it had been a war out in the streets in Atlanta and wounded soldiers had been shipped in from all four corners of the city.

"Cool!" Mars exclaimed. "You hungry?"

"Nah," Forrest replied. "Too tired to be hungry."

"Too bad. Auntie Sadie cooked the best sesame chicken and vegetables. She even made spring rolls!" Mars said.

"Put some up for me and I'll eat it tomorrow," requested Forrest as he walked slowly down the hall. His feet felt like they weighed seventy-five pounds each.

"I'll take your bag," Mars said as he pulled Forrest's backpack off of his shoulder and put it on his.

"Thanks," Forrest replied.

"You're welcome Daddy," Mars responded as he led Forrest to his bedroom.

As soon as Forrest reached the threshold of his bedroom door, he stopped and exhaled gruffly. All he wanted to do was to climb into his bed, but Sadie was sound asleep next to Sky who looked frailer than he had ever seen; a mere shadow of her former self. Her beautiful hair was thin and dry. Her lips looked like serpent scales. Her ashen skin lay across her bones like a dried-up washcloth over a shower rail.

Mars dropped his father's backpack on the fainting couch, at the foot of the bed, and exited the room.

Forrest cleared his throat loudly.

Sadie opened her eyes.

Forrest stood in the doorway with an exasperated look on his face.

She sat up and slipped her feet into her shoes.

"Hey," she whispered sleepily.

"Hey," Forrest replied. "Thanks for staying late."

"No problem," Sadie said as she wiped the sleep from her eyes and ran her fingers through her curly hair.

"How is she?" Forrest asked leaning against the doorpost.

"As well as expected," Sadie responded as she stood up and picked up her purse from the nightstand.

"I really appreciate you looking after her when I have to work long shifts," Forrest said.

"That's my job," Sadie replied with a faint smile. She bent over and kissed Sky on the forehead. "I better get going."

"I'm sure James will be happy to see you," Forrest said feeling guilty that Sadie had been spending so much time at his home. She even took leave from work to help take care of Sky because Sky refused to be in a hospital.

"James has been working a lot. By the time I get home, he is usually asleep," said Sadie walking towards the bedroom door.

Forrest stepped to the side to let her out of the room and followed her down the hall.

"You know I can get the nurse to work longer hours when I am not here. I feel awful that you are missing so much time with your family," Forrest said. "You wouldn't have to sacrifice so much time."

"I don't mind, and my family understands. Besides, Sky is my family. Being with Sky in her most vulnerable state is the least I can do. She has been through so much with me," Sadie said.

"Thanks for cooking for my children," Forrest said changing the subject. He knew that Sadie would never allow him to hire someone to do what she felt was her job.

"My pleasure," she yawned.

Forrest opened the front door and Sadie walked out of the house. He watched her get into her car and drive off into the night. He closed the door and then went into each one of his children's bedroom to inquire about their day before he retired to his own room and settled in next to his dying wife.

XLIV

Venus walked down the hallway, carefully stepping over studying students and navigating through undergraduates whispering sweet nothings against the walls. She made it to the end of the hallway, pulled her phone out, and scrolled through her text messages to verify that she was standing in front of the correct door. She was. She knocked three times and waited. In less than a minute, the door swung open and Venus stepped backward; fear zigzagging through her entire body. The boy standing before her looked like a zombie; pale veiny skin, see through eyes, and smelled of rotten meat.

"Is Khalid here?" she stuttered. She took two more steps backward and prepared herself to run.

"Why yes," Belial answered; a haunting grin on his face. "You look like you've seen a ghost."

Khalid brushed past Belial and greeted Venus nervously with a kiss on the cheek. She hesitantly kissed him back.

"This is my roommate Belial," Khalid introduced. "Belial, this is my friend Venus."

Venus held on to Khalid's arm as if her life depended on it. She nodded her greeting unable to force hello from her mouth.

Belial looked Venus up and down; his dark tongue licking his thin cracked lips.

"Quite beautiful," he purred. "Nice to meet you dear," Belial chortled. "I have heard so many things." He inhaled, moving his head in a circular motion, smelling her like an animal.

Khalid stepped in front of Venus using his body as a shield, protecting her from Belial's breath, his violating eyes, and his crass sniffing.

"She is the one," Belial announced. I can smell it!"

"One what?" Khalid asked between his teeth.

"The one for you. You both have hearts as cold as a corpse," Belial cackled and drummed his blue tipped fingers. "Soulmates!"

Embarrassment turned Khalid's face red. He wanted to choke Belial for behaving so stupidly and he also wanted to choke himself because he believed that the demon's words were true. Khalid felt that Venus was his soulmate. Everything about her was perfect for him. Venus was beautiful, bold, fearless, and vicious; truly intoxicating in every way a girl could be.

"Chill out," Khalid warned Belial.

Belial laughed; his breath filling the air like a stink bomb.

"You want to come in?" Khalid asked.

"I'm not sure," Venus answered placing her hand over her nose. She leaned in and whispered into Khalid's ear, "What's wrong with him?"

"Everything, my dear," Belial answered for Khalid. "Everything!"

Venus pulled herself closer to Khalid. There was no way that Belial should have been able to hear what she had said.

"It was a pleasure to meet you beautiful one," Belial cajoled as he exited the doorway and scurried down the hall; his shadow following an eerie distance behind.

"What the hell?" Venus whispered under her breath not processing what she had just seen.

"Come in," Khalid invited. "He should be gone for a while. I told him that you were coming over."

Venus walked into the room and froze as soon as her eyes met Turiel's.

"What is that Khalid?" she asked as she backed slowly towards the door.

"It's a statue of my dad," Khalid answered.

"Can I touch it?" she asked walking towards the angel standing near Khalid's bed.

"I wouldn't advise that. It just received a fresh layer of gold paint," he lied.

"It's so beautiful and lifelike," Venus mumbled mesmerized by the angel. She leaned close into its face and swore that she felt warmth emitting from it.

"Step back," Khalid demanded.

Venus ignored him completely. She walked a circle around the angel admiring the lifelike quality of its wings, its robes, its hair.

"Incredible," she mumbled inhaling the faint scent of myrrh emitting from the angel.

"Who made this?" she asked letting her fingers trace the air surrounding it. "It looks so real." A lust for touching it churned in her heart.

"Belial," Khalid answered pulling Venus away from Turiel. "Seriously, leave it alone. Did you come to see me or what?

Venus reluctantly tore her eyes away from the angel and looked into Khalid's eyes.

"Your roommate is creepy as hell. There is something real wrong with him. How can you sleep with him and that statue in the room?" Venus asked sitting on Khalid's bed.

"Believe me, it's hard," he answered sitting down beside her. He grabbed her hand and kissed the back of it.

She awkwardly smiled.

"What's that for?" Venus asked.

"I want to thank you for taking up for me in front of the police. You stood by me even when the girl who claimed that she loved me wanted me to give myself over to the police," he answered. "The only other woman who ever fought for me like that was my grandmother. May she rest in peace."

"You're welcome Khalid. I did for you what I know you would have done for me," Venus said.

"You think so?" he asked with one eyebrow raised.

"I know so," she snapped.

"You're right. I would have done the same." He paused and kissed the back of her hand again. He said looking into her eyes, "Venus, I've had a crush on you since we were kids. No one understands me like you do. I can tell you anything."

"I feel the same," Venus interrupted.

"I want you to be my girlfriend," he said. "I love you."

"I love you too, Khalid," she responded.

"Will you be my girl?" he asked again.

"Yes," she whispered. "I would love to be your girlfriend."

Khalid grabbed the back of Venus's head and pulled her face to his. He kissed her softly on the lips and pulled back. She reciprocated pulling him forward again. They kissed for a moment then sat there quietly holding hands. He could tell by the way she kissed that he must have been her first kiss. His heart leapt. He wanted to be her first everything.

"Why are you smiling?" Venus asked suspiciously.

"No reason," Khalid responded, a knowing half grin on his face.

"Whatever," Venus snapped.

She turned her eyes back to the angel. Its eyes were locked on her. A chill ran through her. Venus tried to force the fear away, but it settled within her marrow.

"How is your mother?" he asked, turning her face to his.

Venus laid her head on his shoulder and sat in silence a little longer. There was something about the angel that made her terribly uncomfortable. Thinking about her mother only made the feeling worse.

"Are you okay?" he asked.

"No," Venus answered.

Khalid put his arm around her shoulder. She nestled into his armpit.

"I'm always here if you need me," he whispered kissing her on her forehead.

"Likewise," she responded, jumping up from the bed. Venus had suddenly grown tired of all the sentimental exchanges. "Let's get out of here. It's freaking depressing and that angel is creeping me out! I could have sworn that that thing's hand was in a different position last time I looked."

Khalid laughed. He grabbed her hand, and they left the room.

XLV

The sound of the ceiling fan blended with Sadie's snores as James sat up in bed reading. He closed his book and laid it on the nightstand before turning to kiss his sleeping wife on the forehead. Sadie stirred, then proceeded to snore. James ran his fingers through her silver hair and kissed her neck softly. She mumbled something under her breath and the snoring continued. James pushed her from her side to her back and pulled up her nightgown; sprinkling soft kisses up her thighs.

Sadie's eyes slowly opened as his lips moved into the crease of her upper thigh.

"I'm so tired, baby," Sadie mumbled; catching his face before he began to devour her.

James looked into her eyes and shook his head loose. He attempted to kiss her sacred oasis, but she stopped him by shifting her hips to the side.

James sprang up from the bed so mad that he could spit.

"I ain't doing this no mo'!" he yelled like a kid who lost a neighborhood race for the eighth time.

"Doing what?" Sadie asked; sitting up in bed. "It's two o'clock in the morning. I'm tired!"

"I ain't doin' this no sex for a year b.s. no mo'!" James huffed.

"It's only been a week James. Don't you think you are being a bit overly dramatic?" Sadie replied with her lips twisted and arms folded.

"Nope! With you, a week can turn to a month and a month to a year and I ain't goin' through that again!" James yelled. "I ain't gone do it!"

"Baby, I will never let that happen again. Come back to bed," Sadie welcomed him by holding up the cover inviting him to get under.

James reluctantly climbed into bed.

"Well, let's do it then," James said pulling up her gown.

Sadie laughed. She wiggled away from him.

"Tomorrow night," Sadie promised.

Anger lit up James's face.

"You ain't gone be here tomorrow night! You ain't never home. You act like Sky is all that matta'! When was the last time you had a conversation with Uriel or ate dinner with me? Don't make promises that you can't keep!" James huffed.

"Don't be like that," Sadie begged. "I know I've been busy lately, but you have to know that circumstances call for that. I'm truly tired. I will make it up to you. I promise. Sky needs me right now and…"

James cut her off by putting his big hand in her face like a black stop sign.

"Whateva! Our whole relationship you put somebody else in front of me! Lovin' you is like tryin' to fill up a cup wit' a big hole in the bottom! I had to sit back and accept it when you were bonin' a poltergeist, then I had to be second to that demon Khalid, and now I'm runner up to Sky. When she die, whose next?"

Sadie's eyes stretched wide. She couldn't believe that he had just said that. It was not like him to be so cruel. She was speechless, tearless, utterly appalled by his words.

James didn't care. He was tired of respecting everyone's feelings but his own. If she cried, he would just have to tune it out like he tuned out the sound of the ceiling fan. He turned his back to her, yanked the cover off her shoulders, and pulled it up over his shoulders.

Sadie sat in silence for a long moment. James was hurt and in turn he had hurt her. She instantly forgave him. She kissed the top of his head and slowly pushed his shoulder down until he was lying on his back. His anger contorted face softened. She climbed on top of him and allowed herself to be penetrated as she laid her head against his chest and pretended that everything was okay.

XLVI

A nurse entered Sky's bedroom with a clean set of linens in her small hands. The short, pretty nurse helped Forrest to sit Sky on the fainting couch, so she could change her bedsheets. After the nurse finished, Sky was helped back to bed and tucked in.

"Thanks Nurse Toy," Sky whispered, her voice cracking with every word.

"You're welcome sweetie," the brown nurse replied with a sad smile; her curly braids draping her shoulders. She brushed Sky's hair down and offered her something to drink.

Sky declined as her face twisted into a mask of pain.

"How are you feeling? Do you need a little more pain medicine?" the nurse asked.

Sky nodded, and the nurse gave her another dose of morphine.

Forrest watched from the other side of the room like someone staring at a strange piece of art. The woman lying in his bed was not the woman he married. He had no idea who that decrepit woman was, but he loved her nonetheless because he knew his wife was tucked deep inside that withering body full of sickness and death. It was only a matter of time before Sky would break free from her fleshly tomb.

"Dr. Cohen, can I talk to you in the other room for a moment?" Nurse Toy asked looking up at him like a child to an adult; her petite frame being dwarfed by his tallness.

"Call me Forrest," he insisted.

"I rather not," Nurse Toy said always maintaining an air of professionalism which prevented her from becoming too attached to her patients and their families.

Not taking the nurse's reaction personally, Forrest led the way to the living room.

"What is it Nurse Toy?" he asked; arms folded and eyes intense.

"Sky's body has begun to cool," the nurse answered.

"What does that mean?" he asked knowing very well what it meant; for in the last few nights he felt the iciness of her flesh when he slept next to her. He was a doctor. He knew. He just needed to hear the words aloud. Maybe then they would seem real. Maybe then he could accept them.

"Sky is dying," the nurse answered. "She's been talking to her deceased parents. I'm afraid that she may not make it to the weekend."

"What do you mean?" Jupiter asked stepping into the room. He had unintentionally heard what the nurse had said while he was making a sandwich in the kitchen.

Fear filled Forrest. He wanted to deliver the bad news himself. He did not want his children to learn about their mother's fatal prediction by overhearing.

Tears streamed from Jupiter's eyes. A guttural moan escaped his lips and bounced from the walls like a basketball. Soon his wailing drew his siblings from their rooms.

"What's going on?" Venus asked removing her earbuds from her ears. "Why are you crying like that?"

Earth and Mars stood quietly waiting for answers.

Nurse Toy mouthed that she was sorry, excused herself from the room, and went back to check on Sky.

"What's wrong with Jupiter, Daddy?" Mars asked.

"She's dead, isn't she?" Venus screamed with her fists balled and eyes fierce.

"Mama's dead?" Earth cried.

"No!" Forrest yelled over his wailing children. "You mother is not dead."

"Then why is he crying?" Venus pointed to Jupiter who was slumped over the dining room table like he had been shot.

Forrest opened his mouth, but nothing came out. How could he possibly comfort his children by telling them that their mother was alive, but she may be dead by the weekend?

"Tell us what's wrong!" Venus belched. She knocked down a dining room chair.

Forrest ignored her outburst and dropped down on the nearest couch. His two youngest children ran to him and draped themselves across his lap as the oldest two bawled like babies.

"What's wrong Jupiter?" Venus asked; gnashing her teeth.

"I overheard the nurse tell dad that mom probably was going to die before the weekend," he bawled.

Venus turned and ran from the room. A second later her bedroom door slammed so hard that it sounded like it came off the hinges.

"Mama's going to die?" Mars asked his father.

"I don't know. There is a possibility that your mother may pass away soon, but no one knows when. Death is not predictable, baby," Forrest answered.

Earth leapt up from the sofa and ran out of the front door as fast as her legs could carry her; the concrete scratching her bare feet; her red hair blowing in the wind like a Russian flag; unafraid of the darkness around her; ignoring the call of her father behind her. Uriel had promised her that God would not take her mother. She needed to see if Uriel kept his promises.

XLVII

Red hands. Bright red hands like paint dipped weapons of destruction. Khalid's red hands touched, and bodies fell. Red covered forearms and elbows. A cackling imp sat perched upon a light post watching the bodies fall and red reach Khalid's shoulders. He held his hands up to the imp and the imp shook its head from side to side. Khalid growled full of vexation as red coated his shoulders. He stopped walking and the imp descended upon his head; its body forcing Khalid's neck to bend unnaturally. CRACK!

Uriel sprang up so quickly that he almost fell out of bed. Laborious breathing impaired his reason as he fought hard to catch his breath and slow his heart rate.

"Uriel!" James called from another room. "Uriel get out here!" he yelled.

Uriel got out of bed and exited his room wearing only boxers and a Prince and the Revolution t-shirt.

"Yeah," he answered his father through sleep heavy eyes.

"You got company," James said looking at his watch. It was almost ten 'o clock. "You may wanna put on some pants," James suggested as Earth stood in the middle of the living room drenched in sweat and staring right at Uriel.

"I'll let yo' parents know that you here," James said to Earth.

Earth nodded her head slowly.

James pegged her for being weird and returned to his bedroom to notify Forrest of his daughter's whereabouts.

Uriel ran back into his bedroom and returned to the living room in a pair of basketball shorts.

"Are you okay?" he asked Earth who was still standing in the same spot he left her.

Earth shook her head from side to side; her hair now a tangled afro crowning her head and upper back like a cobra neck.

"Sit down with me," Uriel invited.

She followed him to the sofa and sat so close to him that she was almost on his lap.

"Mama is going to die," she said slowly.

"No, she's not," Uriel rebutted. "It is not God's will for her to die yet. Auntie Sky has a long life ahead of her. She will die old, in her right mind, and sleeping in her bed surrounded by her children, her grandchildren, and her great grandchildren."

"How do you know?" Earth asked; her eyes praying for assurance.

"I just do," Uriel answered. "I feel it in my heart."

"You haven't seen her. If you saw her, you wouldn't say that. She looks like a skeleton. Her skin is discolored, and her hair is almost gone. My dead grandmother sits on her bed and watches her sleep at night." Earth explained. "My mother is dying."

Uriel wrapped his arm around her shoulder and sat in silence. There was nothing more that he could say. All he knew was when he prayed for Sky's recovery, his spirit told him that God had heard his prayer, and everything would be fine. Selfishly, he was not worried about Sky. Uriel was confident about Sky's recovery. Khalid was the one who worried him excessively. Uriel would go visit him the first chance he got.

"I need you to see her," Earth said. "I need you to."

"I'll ask my mom to drive us there," Uriel said as he jumped up from the sofa and headed to his parents' room.

Sadie and James returned with Uriel to the living room.

"What's going on honey?" Sadie asked. "Why are you here so late?"

"Mama is dying. The nurse said so. I couldn't stand being there, so I ran here," Earth admitted.

"That's a long way to run. It musta took you forty-five minutes to get here. We'll take you home," James said picking up his car keys.

The four exited the house and piled into James's car.

Sadie sat silently in the front seat with tears rolling down her face.

Guilt seized James. He had said so many cruel things about Sky and now his words were tearing him apart. He loved Sky like a sister and didn't want anything to happen to her. James reached over and placed his hand on top of Sadie's as they turned down the road.

XLV|||

Sky hated to sleep with the lights off. Everyone knew this about her. Images in her mind were way too bright for the darkness. They became a part of the fabric of reality and that was too much for Sky to bear so she always kept the hall light on or the bathroom light. That way, the darkness would never be complete, and the phantoms could not come.

Sky opened her eyes and there was still darkness. Instantly she knew that Nurse Toy had forgotten to leave the light on; again. She elbowed Forrest until he awoke.

"What?" he grumbled, pushing her elbow away and turning on his side.

"Someone turned off the light," Sky whispered. "I can't see."

Forrest got up out of the bed and turned on the bathroom light. He cracked the bathroom door so that the light would not flood the room completely and returned to bed.

"Thank you," Sky whispered.

Forrest mumbled and went into a coma.

Sky turned her back to her sleeping husband and tried to will herself back to sleep. She was not successful. There were way too many thoughts occupying her mind. She had heard Nurse Toy's prediction. Despite the nurse's desire for discretion, her naturally loud voice carried throughout the house when she spoke. Sky knew death was coming but had no idea that its plane had already landed, and it was on the way to her house.

She allowed her eyes to focus on a painting she painted when she and Forrest first moved into their home in New York. The self portrait of Sky and Forrest intertwined in a kiss used to sit above their bed in New York City, now it hung over the fireplace in their bedroom.

A soft touch on the shoulder broke Sky's train of thought. She turned to face her husband and was confronted by her mother standing next to Forrest's side of the bed.

Sky blinked her eyes hoping that the spirit would go away but every time she opened them, her mother remained.

Sky's mother smiled and held out her hand.

Sky shook her head declining the offer.

Her mother made her way around the bed and stood before Sky. Sky grabbed Forrest's arm and wrapped it around her as if it was a force field against the dead.

"Why are you here?" Sky whispered; her vocal cords too tender to scream. "I'm not ready yet."

Her mother smiled a sad smile. She tapped her finger on her wrist indicating that time was up.

Sky pushed herself into Forrest until he fell off the bed and hit the floor with a loud thump.

"What's going on?" Forrest huffed; rubbing the side of his head. He got up and sat on the edge of the bed.

Sky said nothing as her eyes remained affixed on her mother.

"What are you looking at?" Forrest asked following her gaze. He saw nothing but their furniture. "Sky!" he shook her by the leg.

In the dim lighting, Sky's face looked skeletal and sharp, her eyes sunken in, her collar bones protruding. She looked like Santa Muerta, the Mexican death goddess.

A chill ran down Forrest's back.

Sky turned from her mother to Forrest then back to her mother who was slowly fading into the backdrop of the room.

"Did you see her?" Sky whispered.

"See who?" Forrest asked trying not to envision Our Lady of Holy Death.

"My mama," she cried.

Forrest wrapped his arms around Sky and held her tight.

"You were dreaming, baby. There's no one in here but me and you," he assured her as he kissed the top of her balding head knowing that her days were numbered.

XLVIX

"I don't know what you are looking for!" Khalid yelled to the top of his lungs into the face of his decaying roommate; the dead body of a young white male lying at his feet like a stuffed animal.

Frustration completely filled Khalid. He was at a lost for what Belial wanted for spiritual possession. There was only a matter of time before missing people would be linked to Khalid. Suspicion of him by the police department was already high. Now, Khalid was responsible for another dead student.

"I am looking for perfection," Belial spat, "not the deficient offerings you have been bringing me."

"What's wrong with him? He's young, in good health, decent looking, and strong," Khalid bellowed. "He was a member of my swim team, so he was athletic as well."

"He also had a major opioid addiction which affected his liver. He would have killed himself if you hadn't killed him," Belial said crossing his veiny arms.

"How am I supposed to know that?" Khalid asked genuinely perplexed. "I am not a doctor or a psychic!"

"That's where you are wrong," Belial hissed. "You have powers that you haven't even tapped into. You could have scanned his thoughts to discover his recreational activities."

Khalid kicked the dead man to the side and plopped down on his bed like a child throwing a tantrum.

"I give up!" Khalid declared.

"Fine. I will send the angel into the abyss. The deal is off," Belial said as he opened his box and released a hoard of flying lights. The lights covered Turiel from head to toe.

"No!" Khalid hollered. "Don't hurt him! Please. I will find what you are looking for. I promise."

"You better!" Belial hissed; waving his hand.

The luminescent creatures ascended from the angel and went back into the box.

Pale spots speckled the angel like magical pox. His face looked broken and afraid. The chains on Turiel's wrists grew tighter until it cut into his statuesque flesh.

"Stop!" Khalid begged.

He truly hated the demon. The first thing he planned on doing after Turiel was free was to kill Belial slowly and painfully and to cast it into hell where he belonged.

"What are you waiting for boy? Go!" Belial hissed like a viper; his shadow seemed to tower over its master as a threat to Khalid. "And take that body with you!"

"You take care of it!" Khalid retorted as he rushed from the room. He wasn't going to risk dragging a body out of the dorms in broad day light. He prayed that no one saw the dead student walk in with him in the first place.

Khalid exited the dorm building and made his way towards the gymnasium. He figured that there had to be at least one healthy athlete there that was not a drug addict or addicted to steroids. Before he could cross the yard, Yvette stepped into his path like his mother used to when he tried to leave the house without her permission. Thoughts of his mother made his stomach queasy. Sadie would be horrified if she found out what he had gotten himself into.

"Hey, Khalid," Yvette greeted with eyes wide and full of wanting. She wore his favorite dress, no makeup, and her braids up in a bun like he liked it. Her toes were freshly painted, and she smelled of pumpkin cookies; his favorite lotion of hers.

He looked at her, said nothing, and attempted to walk around her.

She grabbed his arm; her grasp so tight that her short nails dug into his arm.

He pulled away violently almost knocking her to the ground.

"Why you acting like this?" Yvette cried. "You don't love me no more?"

"I never loved you in the first place. Why are you talking to me? I have somewhere to be!" he growled and tried to walk away again.

She stepped into his path once more.

"Well, I love you and you just can't dismiss me like I don't mean nothin'!" Yvette cried. "We've been together since you came here. I've been by your side through everything! Even when you hurt me by dealing with other girls!"

"That was your choice," Khalid shot back.

"Please give me another chance," Yvette wept. She fell to her knees and wrapped her arms around his legs.

Nearby students gawked at her act of desperation, many embarrassed for him, making Khalid more irritated.

Khalid side stepped out of her grasp and walked away.

Shamelessly, she followed him screaming and carrying on like a crazed juvenile.

Witnessing students shook their heads disapprovingly as they pointed and discussed the scene unfolding before their eyes.

Khalid continued to ignore Yvette and quickly walked around to the back of the gym.

"Listen to me!" Yvette screamed. "Please!"

He walked on as if she was nothing more than a buzzing fly trying to get swatted.

She picked up a rock and threw it as hard as she could. With an audible thump, it hit him in the back of the head. Blood ran down the back of his head; crimson lines running down his neck, and unto the collar of his t-shirt. Khalid touched the back of his head and brought his scarlet fingertips into sight. Like a bull, the red infuriated him. He looked at her; bearing teeth like a rabid dog.

"Didn't I tell you to leave me alone?" Khalid croaked; running towards her full speed. He grabbed her by the neck and slammed her body into a brick wall so hard that her breath left her mouth in a heavy gust of spittle and moans.

"I'm sorry," Yvette blubbered. "I didn't mean to hurt you."

Drool ran down her mouth as his hands covered her entire throat. Hissing escaped from her lips like a pierced balloon.

Khalid squeezed her neck like a vise. Bones cracked. Yvette's eyes went blank. Khalid picked her up, threw her over his shoulder, and began walking back towards his dorm as fast as his legs could carry him. Every time someone's curiosity peaked, he slapped Yvette across the butt and pretended that she was laughing. He took the stairs to his room because students hardly ever used them. He arrived at his room and realized that he had left his key inside. He visually searched the hallway ensuring that there was no one around; then, knocked on the door. There was no answer. Two doors down, the door opened. A student stuck his head out of the door, issued a smile of recognition, exited his room, and approached Khalid.

"Hey Khalid!" the handsome young man greeted looking curiously at Yvette's limp body draped across Khalid's shoulder.

Khalid's heart began to thump violently against his ribcage. The student speaking to him was well liked. Khalid would hate to have to kill him if he realized that Yvette was not breathing. He hoped the guy would just go back to his room.

"What's up wit' ya girl?" the student asked with marijuana between his lips. Smoke circled his face as he spoke. The smell filled the hallway quickly.

"She's lit," Khalid answered. "I told her not to take pills from people she didn't know. You think she listened? This knucklehead took a crap load of pills and washed it down with some liquor. I saw her in the lobby and decided to bring her up to rest."

"Wow. That's wild," the student said losing interest in the high girl. "Give her some coffee and send her back where she came from. Your new girl is much hotter!" he said referring to Venus. He had seen her with Khalid a while back and instantly developed a crush on her.

"Bet," Khalid said fist bumping the student with his free hand. "Holla at you later. She's getting heavy."

The student walked away right before Khalid's dorm room door swung open. He entered and dropped Yvette at Belial's feet.

"You can't be serious. I'm beginning to think that you are toying with me and I do not appreciate being toyed with," Belial mumbled and stepped over the dead girl. He opened his box and summoned his light creatures. They covered the girl. In minutes, Yvette was no more.

Khalid headed back out of the door to scout out his next victim. After high school, He expected that college would change him into a party animal, a serious adult, maybe even a bit of a philosopher, but never did he think it would turn him into a bona fide serial killer.

L

"Are you okay?" Forrest asked Sky; still rocking her in bed. The feel of her hair was like dry grass to his chest.

"I'm telling you, Mama was really here," Sky swore. "I saw her."

"Okay, baby," Forrest agreed. "I believe you."

He did believe her. It was very common for dying people to see dead people around them.

The doorbell rang.

"Who is that?" Sky asked looking at the clock. It was nearly eleven at night.

"Probably James bringing Earth home," Forrest answered.

He pulled on a pair of pajama pants and a t-shirt. Although Sky was sick and was unable to be physically intimate with him, he still enjoyed feeling her close to his naked body as they slept.

"Why would Earth be with James?" Sky asked genuinely perplexed.

"She ran out of the house after hearing about what Nurse Toy said about you leaving us," Forrest admitted.

Sky frowned. She instantly hated Forrest's words. Leaving sounded like she was voluntarily dying. She was not leaving them. She had no choice in the matter. Cruel fate was taking her away from her family.

"Why didn't you go after her?" Sky asked angrily not understanding why Earth would be allowed to literally run the streets at night. Sky wished she had the strength to get out of bed to give Earth a piece of her mind.

"I knew where she was going," Forrest said. "She needed space. I knew she would go to Uriel's."

"Not acceptable! Anything could have happened to her on the way there. Atlanta is one of the biggest child trafficking hubs in the world and you allowed our daughter to jog across town because she needed space?" Sky yelled as loud as she could. It sounded like a forceful whisper. She tried to sit up but was too weak.

"I'll be back," Forrest said and left the room.

He understood that she was mad but arguing was not an option. He refused to spend the last days with his wife in discontent. Forrest opened the front door and invited the Tucker family inside.

"Thank you for bringing Earth home. Sorry that she disturbed you guys," Forrest apologized.

"Boy stop!" Sadie exclaimed. "Earth is family! She can come to our home anytime. Uriel is like a brother to her."

Uriel blushed. That was the furthest thing from the truth. He looked at Earth as a lot of things, but a sister was not one of them.

James and Forrest instantly recognized the look on Uriel's face and laughed under their breaths.

"Thanks again for bringing her back. I'm a bit too tired to entertain. We can talk tomorrow if you want," Forrest said.

"A'ight!" James replied while throwing his head back in agreement.

Sadie headed towards the door.

"I want to see Auntie Sky," Uriel said looking into Earth's wet eyes. Seeing her unhappy made every part of his body feel miserable.

"It's late. I'm sure Sky is resting," Sadie said. "She needs all the rest that she can get. She's not doing very well."

"Please let him see her," Earth begged. "He can make her better."

"Oh, honey," Sadie sighed as she caressed Earth's face. "I know very strange things have occurred in my family; things that are not easily explained, but there is nothing that Uriel can do. He doesn't have the power to heal. No one does. I'm sorry if he led you to believe that he could change things."

Forrest looked at Uriel with annoyance. There was nothing the child could do to make his wife better, and he resented the boy for making his daughter believe otherwise.

"Please, Daddy," Earth begged burying her face in his chest. "Please."

"What do you think Uriel can do?" James asked. "Do you want him to pray for her?"

Earth nodded.

"Uriel go in and pray for Sky if you wish," Forrest said.

"Yes sir," Uriel responded walking away, and heading to see Sky.

Uriel knocked on Sky's open bedroom door.

"May I come in?" Uriel asked.

"Of course," Sky invited. "It's so good to see you. You look more like your daddy every day."

Uriel walked into the bedroom straight to her bedside.

"May I pray for you?" he asked not wasting time on small talk.

"Of course, sweetheart," Sky said. "I need all the prayer I can get."

Uriel fell to his knees; his elbows resting on her bed and his head pressed against his folded hands. He prayed silently for a while then he placed one hand upon her head, the warmth from his palm comforting her instantly, and held her other hand. He began to pray aloud. The words surrounded Sky like a blanket. Uriel pled and wrestled with God with his tongue. Tears streamed down both their faces as Uriel asked for Sky's healing. His hands grabbed her tightly as he offered supplications to the Lord. Uriel wailed and prayed so loud that the others came to stand in the doorway to see what was transpiring.

Earth saw her deceased grandmother on her knees next to Uriel with her hands lifted in the air and her eyes staring at the ceiling. Prayers silently rose from her lips.

Uriel asked for God's power to work through him. He begged for God's mercy to wash over Sky.

Embarrassment and disbelief urged Sadie to rush in and interrupt, but she resisted and remained where she was out of love for her son and friend for she knew that her personal feelings were not important. Prayer was what Sky wanted and needed at the moment.

James bowed his head and prayed with them as Earth and Forrest speechlessly looked on.

Sky wept. She began to praise God. Her whispery voice slowly became strong and loud. Color came back to her ashen skin. She could feel the blood circulating through her veins renewing her from the inside out; transforming cancer cells into whole cells, cells as perfect as the ones at birth. Every molecule of her flesh devoured every infected cell, bacteria, virus that produced sickness, accelerated death, or promoted deficient health and morphed into cellular perfection. Her sweat dampened skin glowed with new life.

Sky's mother kissed her on the forehead and disappeared. She felt the warmth of the kiss and shouted hallelujah for she knew that her mother's spirit had gone back to its proper domain.

Sky sat up in bed and sang God's praises. She began to walk around the room in a trance of praise and thanksgiving.

Uriel cried out in thanksgiving as he witnessed the strength come back to her body.

Tears streamed down Sadie and Forrest's eyes as they watched Sky begin to dance and sing. Her skeletal body floated through the room on hind's feet. Her voice sang in a language divine.

Forrest, Sadie, James, and Earth watched with eyes stretched; hand on chests, mouths ajar in utter disbelief of what they were witnessing.

Sky seemed whole and healed and was hollering hallelujah. Moments later, believers and unbelievers alike joined in the celebration. For they all witnessed what was dying regain new life.

LI

Uriel leaned against the train window and watched the city zoom by in flashes of architecture and mother nature comingling in a blur of city life. In two more stops, he would be near Khalid's school. The sky darkened. Rain began to pelt the windows. Uriel searched his backpack for his pocket-sized umbrella. It wasn't in his bag. His mother must have taken it after misplacing hers again.

The train stopped, and Uriel exited quickly before the crowd swallowed him. He ran through the station and out onto the street. He didn't break his stride until he arrived at Khalid's dorm. He made his way to Khalid's room and banged on the door like he was the police.

The door swung open.

"Why are you trying to break the door down?" Khalid asked his soaking wet brother. "Come in."

Uriel crossed the threshold; his t-shirt sticking to his chest and his arms shivering.

"Let me get you some fresh clothes," Khalid said as he walked to his dresser and pulled out a few items and tossed them to Uriel.

Uriel's eyes locked on the angel standing between Belial's desk and empty bed.

"What is he doing here?" Uriel stammered.

"Long story," Khalid answered. "It's just a sculpture."

"No, it's not," Uriel said grabbing the clothes. He began to undress; his eyes not leaving the angel. He threw his wet clothes into a pile on the floor and stepped into a pair of jeans. The door swung open.

Belial walked into the room, a perverted grin on his face.

"Who is this handsome specimen?" Belial questioned.

Khalid stepped between Uriel and Belial.

"This is my lil' bro Uriel. Uriel, this is my roommate Belial. He's the weirdo I've been telling you about," Khalid introduced sarcastically.

Uriel pulled a t-shirt over his head and waved at Belial. The chills running down Uriel's spine would not allow him to shake Belial's hand. There was something off about Belial's energy and something demonic about the shadow that trailed him in contradiction to the light source in the room. Uriel prayed silently.

"Pleasure to meet you. You didn't tell me you had a brother, Khalid," Belial cooed; raping Uriel with his eyes.

"I don't tell you lots of things," Khalid snapped. "My family isn't your business."

"You should have told me this one," Belial retorted.

"Whatever. Step off!" Khalid barked.

Uriel cleared his throat; trying to refrain from coughing. The stench of Belial's breath was unfathomable. The smell was unlike anything Uriel had ever smelled before. It was like a mixture of feces and dead possum.

"Show me the campus, Khalid," Uriel requested; prayers still circling through is mind. The fiend Khalid called a roommate was not of this world. Uriel could feel it. Belial's presence was a source of horrible unease.

"Okay, let's go," Khalid agreed. He grabbed his brother's arm and headed out the door.

"Khalid," Belial called out after Uriel had left the room.

"What?" Khalid snapped; turning around to face his roommate; annoyance contorting Khalid's boyish face.

"He's the one," Belial said with a wicked smile.

"No!" Khalid retorted.

"We had a deal!" Belial screeched.

"He is not a part of that deal!" Khalid hissed. "I will get you what you want. Give me time."

Uriel, confused about what was going on, stood quietly in the hallway. Whatever they were arguing about could not be good. Anything dealing with that demon could never be good.

"Khalid," Uriel called breaking up the bickering.

The bickering roommates turned to him.

Khalid said to Uriel, "Go ahead and start walking. I will catch up with you in a minute."

"Okay," Uriel agreed, anxious to get as far away from Belial as he could. He walked down the hall and disappeared around the bend.

Khalid spun around to face Belial.

"No," Khalid growled. "Never."

Belial opened his box and pulled out a dagger. Its pewter handle was adjoined to a jagged and rusty blade decorated with what looked like centuries old blood. He turned to Turiel and grabbed one of his wings. The angel's face tightened. Belial drove the blade between Turiel's wing and back.

The angel dropped to his knees; agony crippling him. Turiel opened his mouth to scream, but nothing came out.

Belial pulled the dagger across the angel's shoulder threatening to sever the entire wing. He looked up at Khalid, who was dumbstruck by the torture of his father.

Belial pulled the dagger out of Turiel's back and licked the blade. Blood ran from the sides of Belial's mouth. His eyes glistened like bicycle reflectors.

"This is only the beginning. Give me the boy!" Belial demanded; his shadow rushing across the room and slamming the door in Khalid's face.

~   ~   ~

"What was that about?" Uriel asked before biting into a sloppy hamburger. Ketchup fell from the bun onto his shirt. Uriel wiped it away with his thumb and licked his thumb clean.

"Just a disagreement," Khalid replied. "Nothing to worry about," he lied.

"You look pretty worried to me," said Uriel; sucking up a straw full of banana pudding milkshake.

Khalid stared out the window watching a group of students congregate around a parked car. They looked happy. Envy filled him. He wished that his life was so carefree.

"What did you want to talk about?" Khalid asked; irritation in his voice. "I know you didn't come this far just to eat. There's plenty of food at home."

Uriel took another bite of his burger and wiped his mouth. He said, "I had another bad dream about you."

Khalid rolled his eyes.

"What's new about that? I have always been the main character of all your nightmares," Khalid remarked.

"I think you should request another room or another roommate. I feel that your roommate is dangerous. He may try to hurt you," Uriel answered, then continued to eat.

"I'll be okay," Khalid replied avoiding his brother's eyes. "If you haven't noticed, there aren't many people in this world who can harm me."

"That's the thing. I don't feel like he's a person," Uriel admitted. "And, he's definitely not of this world."

The waiter dropped the bill on the table and refilled Khalid's cup. After the waiter finished pouring lemonade, he walked away.

Uriel continued, "Did you make some kind of deal with him?"

Khalid said nothing.

"You did. Didn't you?" Uriel asked.

Khalid remained silent.

"I told you before I even met him that he was dangerous. Why would you do that? What is he asking you to do?" Uriel asked; his eyes full of dread.

"Don't worry," Khalid said avoiding his brother's eyes. He continued to stare at the students in the parking lot. One of the girls was almost as beautiful as Venus. He couldn't believe he had never seen her before.

"I will pray for you," Uriel said; worry wrinkled his forehead.

Khalid dropped a twenty-dollar bill on the table and got up. He walked towards the exit and yelled without looking back, "Pray for yourself! Catch a ride share home. I gotta go to class," and walked out of the door.

Uriel pulled his cellphone out of his pocket and requested a ride. He watched his brother walk away. It was the first time Uriel ever detected real fear in Khalid.

L||

Sky sat in the chilly doctor's office waiting for the doctor to come into the examination room. She hated being cold and found it utterly ridiculous that the office felt like a cup of snow could last a week in there. Sky let out a puff of air to see if she could see her breath. She couldn't.

Forrest sat across from her in a poorly cushioned chair; staring at Sky amazed at how beautiful she looked. Her hair had already begun to grow back; her eyes were bright and hopeful; her skin was smooth and even toned. She looked like the woman that he had married so many years ago not the crone who had been taking her place for the last few months.

"Mrs. Cohen, I have your test results," Dr. Rowe said as he walked into the room. He rolled a stool in front of Sky and sat down.

Sky clapped her hands excitedly.

Forrest sighed in admiration of his healthy wife. She seemed completely cured, but the logical part of him felt that she was experiencing some sort of false recovery that would end in a more aggressive regression. Ease would come when he heard the test results.

"I must say, I am puzzled by your results. I have never seen anything like this in my life," the doctor continued. "I compared your before and after charts and reviewed them with my colleagues. We all are in awe at what we found or did not find to be more accurate."

"What do my results say?" Sky asked impatiently. Truth be told, she didn't care about what the results said.

She knew in her heart that she had been healed. She was there only because Forrest insisted upon her getting examined.

The doctor opened Sky's file and sighed.

"Your cell proteins, your DNA and RNA show that there is no cancer present in your body. After your MRI, we saw no traces of anything. It is as if you never had it. Even the side effects of chemotherapy and radiation are gone. What did you do?" the doctor asked.

"I did nothing," Sky answered. "Someone prayed for me and God healed me."

The doctor blinked his eyes slowly trying to figure out how to respond to her answer. Research showed that faith and positive thinking could expedite healing, but his scientific mind could not, better yet, would not accept a full miracle brought on by prayer alone. He placed his file upon his knee and asked, "Are you taking herbs or a new form of treatment that I am not aware of?"

"Nope," Sky responded.

"There has to be a logical explanation," Dr. Rowe replied. "People just don't recover from stage four cancer overnight."

Sky stood up.

"Doc, believe whatever you need to believe to help you sleep at night, but like I told you, God made me well. Take it or leave it," Sky replied as she grabbed her purse and headed out of the door. Forrest followed quickly behind her as she exited the doctor's office almost skipping.

L|||

Khalid walked into his dorm room laboriously dragging a large trunk behind him. He pulled the big leather box into the room and closed the door behind him.

Belial looked up from the book he was reading.

Turiel stared at his son through eyes wrought with pain as his semi-severed wing dangled behind him.

"I got a surprise for you," Khalid said flashing a dashing smile. "I'm sure you're gonna like it!"

Belial threw his legs over the side of his bed as his shadow moved ahead of him.

"Come open it," Khalid waved wearing a proud grin.

Belial lazily walked over to Khalid, skepticism written all over his pasty face. He easily popped the lock on the chest and opened the big box.

Inside a young teenaged boy lay in fetal position; his dark skin was smooth and spotless like Uriel's. Even the bone structure of his face was similar to Uriel's. His body was well built and strong. Beautiful, kinky, West African hair covered his head as he laid there sleeping eternally.

"What is this?" Belial hissed.

"It's your new body," Khalid replied, his smile waning. "He looks just like you wanted. He was young, drug-free, healthy, handsome, and built very much like my brother. I found him at the local high school. He was leaving practice when he crossed my path. Too bad he didn't make it home. I feel horrible for his family, but that's life. Tragic things happen." Khalid lifted and dropped his shoulders.

"I borrowed this box along with a car from a friend of mine, so I could transport the body without notice. I tutored him in math and science, so he happily did me a favor without asking too many questions," he continued.

"But, he is not your brother. No?" Belial replied, his arms crossed and foot tapping.

"No, he is not my brother," Khalid answered. "But look, I killed him by suffocation so that he doesn't have any nasty wounds, and his heart is still in healthy condition."

"I asked for your brother. Did I not?" Belial roared.

"You cannot have my brother," Khalid roared back. "Uriel is not an option. Take this boy and be happy."

Belial zipped across the room. He pulled the ancient dagger from his box and went to work on Turiel. Blood dripped from the angel in so many places that the golden hue of his skin was completely covered by scarlet splashes. Open wounds were filled with salt as the fiend cut deeper into the angel's skin.

"Please stop!" Khalid begged. "Why are you doing this? I gave you what you asked for? Requiring my brother is not a part of our original deal! You said you wanted a new body not a specific body."

"I recall having the option to choose the body!" Belial growled.

"That may be true, but my brother was never a part of your options!" Khalid roared.

Belial called his light creatures to feast upon the wounds like glowing maggots gnawing at decaying flesh.

"Stop!" Khalid wailed. "Please stop. I will see what I can do."

Belial released the angel from his grasp and ordered the feasting lights back into the box. He laid down his dagger and threw a sheet over Turiel's head.

"What an eyesore," Belial exclaimed.

Khalid fell upon his bed in tears. There was no way that he was going to give up his brother and there was no way that he was going to allow Turiel to be killed. He had to find a way to drive the demon out of his roommate. There had to be a way that Khalid could get rid of Belial for good.

L|V

"You have been a hard man to catch up with Mr. Tucker," a portly female detective said; wearing a cheap pantsuit and hair cut like Arsenio Hall's in the early 1990s. Sweat gathered under her wide beige nose. The sound of her thighs rubbing together blended melodiously with the clicks of her kitten heels as she walked across the interrogation room to stand close to the air vent. Her male counterpart sat across the table from Khalid shuffling through a stack of manila folders.

Yvette had been reported missing and Khalid was identified as the last one who had been seen with her.

"I don't see how. I'm in class like every other student. Outside of class, I am in my dorm room or in the library doing homework or at swim practice. Not to mention all the clubs and student organizations I lead. I am the Student Council President, debate team captain, newspaper editor, and I do community service every other weekend with my family. I'm sure you know that I have a full schedule," Khalid responded coolly. He leaned back in his chair and looked from officer to officer.

"Yet, you find time to date. Busy boy," the female officer said.

"Of course," Khalid responded; smiling wide and confidently. "My girlfriend's name is Venus, and trust me, she is a goddess."

The male officer closed the folders in front of him and folded his hands on the table. His pink spotted skin, chipped fingernails, and greasy blonde hair made him look bedraggled and a bit dingy.

"What was your relationship with Miss Hall? Are you aware that you were the last one seen with her?" the male officer asked; his yellow teeth glistening in the lamp light.

"Ironically you were also the last one seen with Duane Hall," the female detective mumbled. Her eyes burrowed through Khalid's skull as if she had some type of x-ray vision that would reveal the truth.

"We used to date," Khalid disclosed.

"Why did you stop dating?" the male officer inquired. He took a sip of coffee and placed the cup back on the table.

"Where is my lawyer?" Khalid asked with a hint of irritation.

"He'll be here soon. Mr. Cummings and your parents are in route," the female detective replied.

"I will answer your questions when they arrive. I'm hungry," Khalid said. He picked up the male officer's pencil and handed it to him. "Write down my order and have one of your flunkies go fetch my food."

The male officer's eyes narrowed. It took every ounce of restraint not to slap Khalid across the face.

"I'll take a barbeque chicken pizza and a bottle of cranberry juice," Khalid requested.

The officer indignantly scribbled Khalid's order down and hopped up so fast from his chair that the chair fell over and hit the floor with a loud thud. Normally he would never give into a suspect's demand, but something made him get up and move when Khalid told him to.

"And hurry up," Khalid snapped. "I don't like cold food."

The officer growled at Khalid's arrogance as he disappeared from the room. Khalid laughed under his breath and pulled out his cell phone to play a game.

The female detective stood in front of the air vent silently watching Khalid. His arrogance, dismissiveness, and lack of emotion regarding his ex-girlfriend's absence secured him as a sociopath in her mind.

The interrogation room door opened and in ran Sadie. James and their lawyer Cecil Cummings followed close behind her.

"Are you okay, baby?" Sadie asked raining kisses on top of Khalid's head. "Did they hurt you?"

James watched from the corner of the room with his arms folded. Half of him wanted to champion Khalid but the other half of him knew that Khalid was well capable of doing everything that he was suspected of.

"I'm okay mom." Khalid answered trying to dodge her wet kisses.

"What have you told them?" Cecil Cummings asked with a light Nigerian accent; his expensive suit fitting his slim body like a glove. A shiny watch glistened from his onyx wrist which led to jeweled fingers holding a snakeskin brief case.

"Only that I used to date Yvette," Khalid replied.

Cecil spun on his heels as if he was doing a dance move and faced the sweating female detective.

"Why was my client being interrogating without me in his presence?" Cecil asked, his heavy voice echoing through the room like the voice of God in a black and white movie.

She twisted her lips and declined to answer.

The male officer reentered the room and tossed a small pizza box and a can of generic brand soda across the table to Khalid. Khalid opened the box and saw a half-eaten slice of meat pizza, a balled-up napkin, and a wad of chewed gum. He laughed. The officer had heart. Khalid would make sure that the officer paid for his drollness later.

Locking eyes with the male officer, Khalid pushed the pizza box and the soda can to the floor. He leaned back in his chair and waited for the interrogation to begin.

The male officer sat down across from Khalid and asked, "When did you and Miss Hall stop dating?"

"Shortly after I was unjustly brutalized by the police," Khalid replied. "Sorry to hear all those offending officers had heart trouble. Maybe if you guys lay off the doughnuts and meat pizza, heart attacks would be less likely." Khalid laughed.

Sadie gasped at her son's cruel remarks. The officers vehemently tightened their lips.

"Why did you two break up?" the male officer asked, his voice trembling uncontrollably with rage.

"We didn't break up. Yvette was never my girlfriend. I stopped hanging with her because she left me to be beaten by police officers," Khalid answered.

"A witness saw you carrying her unconscious body into your room the last night anyone saw her. Why was she unconscious and why was Yvette in your room if you two were no longer friends?" the female detective asked.

"She came to my dorm trying to get me back. She was as high as a kite. She blacked out, and like the gentleman I am, I took her to my room to rest until she was conscious again. She woke up a few hours later and left angrily because my girlfriend was there," Khalid replied. "My roommate and my girlfriend, Venus Cohen, were both there when Yvette stormed out. I haven't seen her since that night."

The male officer scribbled on a notepad as the female detective paced the floor.

"That's interesting," the female detective stated mid-pace.

"What's interesting?" Cecil inquired; sitting down beside his client crossing his long legs putting his pointy toe shoes on display.

James wrapped his arm around Sadie's shoulders as she watched on ill at ease.

"It's interesting that a minor is allowed to be away from home during a school night. We'll have to look into that," the female detective replied. "How old are you Mr. Tucker?"

James started to speak but remembered that the detective was speaking to his son.

"Why?" Khalid hissed. "How old are you?"

The interrogation room door opened, and Venus was escorted in by an officer holding her arm. Fresh scratches lined the side of his face. He flung her into the room and slammed the door behind him. A few seconds later, Forrest and Sky entered the room and stood next to the Tuckers.

"It's getting' kinda crowded," the male officer mumbled. "Some of ya'll gotta go."

James headed towards the door, but Sadie pulled him backward.

"We're not going anywhere without our children," Sadie declared.

The male officer stood up. The female detective put out her hand instructing him to sit back down. Reluctantly, he did.

"How old are you Miss Cohen?" the female detective asked with a shrewd grin on her face.

"Fifteen," Venus spat.

The female detective folded her hands behind her back and began to pace again.

"You are a bit young. What we called jailbait back in my day," she said. "How old are you Mr. Tucker?"

"Sixteen," Khalid replied.

The female detective swallowed her next question. It was obvious that she hadn't studied Khalid's file as extensively as she should have. She was hoping to scare him with a statutory rape charge. She had no idea that the suspect was so young. For the first time, she recognized that Khalid had a baby face. She snatched the folder from the table and verified that he was indeed sixteen years old. The detective turned to Venus.

"When was the last time you saw Yvette Hall?" the female detective asked.

Venus looked at Khalid then to her parents. She took a deep breath and said, "She was in Khalid's dorm room. She left because I came over."

Sky started angrily towards Venus, but Forrest pulled her back. Being sick had put her out of the know with her family. There was no way in the world that Venus would have been able to go out at night if Sky was aware of it. Sky snatched her arm away from Forrest and stormed out of the interrogation room.

"You have already spoken to Khalid's roommate and his girlfriend has corroborated the story. If you have no further questions," Cecil stood up and straightened his blazer. "We are out of here."

The female detective opened the door and allowed Forrest and the Tuckers to exit the room.

Venus stepped into the hallway.

Khalid stepped into the doorway of the interrogation room facing the officers with his back to Venus. The officers stared at him with grimacing faces. The female officer mouthed that it was only a matter of time before they get him.

Khalid's eyes blacked out. He said, "Never contact me or come near me again."

The officers' faces went blank. They nodded slowly, entranced by his swirling black eyes.

"What did you do?" Venus asked seeing the cop's stupor and easy compliance.

Khalid grinned, his face back to normal before he turned to face her.

"Let's go," he said grabbing her hand and interlocking his fingers. They walked out of the police station lagging far behind their parents.

"You know you're in trouble, right?" Khalid said to Venus.

"What's new?" she replied. "I'm always in trouble so I just do what I want to do and face the consequences later."

He grabbed her arm and pulled her around a corner.

"Whatchu doin'?" Venus squealed.

Khalid grabbed her and kissed her softly on the lips.

He whispered, "Thank you for lying for me."

She nodded; looking dreamily into his eyes.

"Let's go!" he laughed and pulled her down the hall, so they could catch up with their parents.

LV

The smell of burgers and ribs floated across the Cohens' back yard. Tornados of fragrant smoke circled the heads of James and Forrest as they prepared food for their loved ones. James, wearing an apron that read "Boss" with the B wearing a crown, flipped a burger and began to lay corn on the cob and shish kebabs on the grill while Forrest, wearing an apron that read "King of the Grill" brushed barbeque sauce on a plate of ribs. Children ran across the yard playing one game or another, and adults danced to music spanning many decades. Neighbors and friends sat around and chatted about everything from business to breakdancing as their red cups overflowed with alcoholic and nonalcoholic beverages.

Sky and Sadie sat on lawn chairs enjoying the last hurrah of warm weather. A chill lingered under the warmth warning them of autumn's imminent return. Venus pouted on the back porch, disappointed that Khalid was not going to attend because of a school debate team tournament. Jupiter sat engulfed in the eyes of a girl that he invited from his school. Mars played gleefully with a couple of neighborhood kids he invited over, and Earth and Uriel sat tucked away under the leaves of a low hanging oak tree contemplating the intricacies of the universe, i.e. high school.

"Shameka Leonard has a crush on you," Earth said while digging her toes into the soft grass.

"Really?" Uriel asked surprised at the revelation. Anyone having a crush on him was unanticipated news, but then again, he looked like his father and women seemed to always notice James when they were out.

"Are you going to ask her out?" Earth asked avoiding his eyes; her voice a pitch higher than usual.

"Naw," Uriel answered. "I'm interested in another girl."

"Who?" Earth asked looking up at the sky.

Clouds formed a dragon with one leg.

"You know her very well. Maybe you can hook us up," Uriel mused. "I'm not sure if she likes me though."

"I'm sure she likes you. Everyone likes you," Earth replied pulling her eyes away from the lame dragon and focusing them on Uriel's.

Uriel smiled. He picked a few thick blades of grass and braided them into a ring.

"The girl I like really likes grass," he said sliding the ring onto Earth's big toe. She threw her head back and laughed.

Uriel leaned in to kiss her on the cheek.

"Uriel!" Sadie yelled across the yard.

Uriel jumped up from the ground like he had gotten caught with his hand in the cookie jar.

"Yes, Ma," he answered.

"Get over here and bring Earth with you," she requested with her eyebrow raised high. Sadie was sure she was witnessing the beginning of a budding romance.

Uriel offered Earth his hand and she accepted it. With a swift pull, she was on her feet and matching his stride towards his mother.

Forrest and Sky stood next to Sadie wearing imbecilic grins. Sky yelled to the other children, "Come over here! We have something to say and everyone needs to hear it."

Completely puzzled by their foolish faces, Uriel and Earth approached them with caution.

"Sit down," Sadie instructed.

Uriel and Earth sat in the chairs adjacent to Earth's parents.

Sky pulled two boxes from under the table. Forrest picked up one and Sky picked up the other.

"I want to thank you for what you did for me," Sky said. Immediately her voice began to tremble. "I said I wouldn't cry," she cried. "But, I'm so happy. You healed my body."

Earth, Venus, and Sadie burst out in tears. The sight of Sky crying drove their emotions over the edge. Even Forrest's nose began to tickle.

"I did nothing," Uriel corrected her. "That was God. I only prayed for you."

"Well, thank you for praying for me!" Sky exclaimed. "Your prayer made all the difference."

"You're welcome, Auntie Sky. I'm sorry I didn't pray with you sooner. Forgive me," Uriel replied.

"You prayed with me when you were supposed to. You needed witnesses to see the greatness of God," Sky said.

Sadie looked away. Her stubbornness forbad her to believe, but the evidence was before her. There was no denying that a great miracle had occurred. Her atheism was dying a slow and painful death and she had no idea how to revive it.

"This is for you," Sky handed Uriel the gift box she was holding.

"You don't have to give me anything," Uriel replied. "You are like my family. Besides, prayers are free. I would pray for anyone."

"Open it," Sky demanded ignoring his modest murmurings.

Uriel opened the box to find two front row tickets to a sold-out rap concert. He jumped up and down like he had won the lottery.

"How did you get these Auntie Sky? The concert has been sold out for months. These tickets must have cost you a fortune! I can't accept these," Uriel sadly replied as he reluctantly held the tickets out for her to take back.

"The hell you can't!" Sky exclaimed. "You will go, have a good time, and take someone special with you."

Uriel threw his arms around Sky and squeezed her until her skinny frame threatened to pop.

"It's my turn," Forrest laughed giving the box to Uriel.

"Thank you for saving my wife and the mother of my children," Forrest said, a tear rolling down his cheek.

"It wasn't…" Uriel started.

"You were the catalyst for change. It was you that visited her, and it was you that asked for healing and it was to you that God listened. So, thank you for all that you did." Forrest said trying not to sob like his blubbering wife next to him.

"You're welcome Uncle Forrest," Uriel replied. "I'm glad I could help."

Forrest handed him the box and Uriel opened it to find the most exclusive pair of sneakers on the market. As a sneaker lover, the sight of them almost knocked Uriel unconscious.

Uriel let out a high pitch scream and spun around in a circle.

"Wait until Khalid sees these!" he howled.

The laughter of family and friends joined his celebratory whooping as Uriel howled with all his might.

LVI

In high school, cafeteria food was a step up from dog food, but Khalid found that the food on his college campus was pretty tasty. A huge variety of delectable delights from stir fry and salads to fried chicken and vegan dishes sat on buffet tables in the middle of the massive dining hall.

Khalid loaded his plate with a mixed green salad with avocado and nuts, and a turkey and cheese sandwich on whole wheat bread. Ice water with lemon rocked on the edge of his tray as he leaned in to pick up a bowl of mixed fruit.

"How are you?" a voiced called from the other side of the buffet table.

Khalid looked up into Hafeeza's solemn face; her eyes pulsing with fear and urgency.

"I'm good. How are you?" Khalid responded unenthusiastically. He placed the bowl of fruit on his tray and found a nearby table to eat his lunch. Hafeeza followed him and sat down.

The cafeteria was nearly empty. Khalid liked it that way. Peace and quiet was something he deeply craved and had little of due to his vigorous school and extracurricular activity schedule. He purposely timed his dinners with the cafeteria closing time. On many occasions, he was the only one there. Unfortunately, this was not one of those times. Khalid looked at Hafeeza with annoyance as he poured olive oil and vinegar on his salad.

"My spirit tells me that you have made a deal with the unworthy one. Things will not end well," she whispered ominously.

"Tell me something I don't know," Khalid replied flippantly as he took a big bite of his sandwich.

"I..." Hafeeza began but her words fell short like an incomplete sneeze.

Belial noisily dropped his tray on the table next to Khalid and sat down. Rare meat sat bleeding on Belial's plate next to three shrimp staring up from his plate like mini monsters.

His shadow stretched across the floor like an ink stain.

"Good day," Belial greeted, his breath smelling like the undercarriage of a defecating horse.

Immediately Khalid's appetite was gone. He dropped his sandwich on his plate and covered his nose with the back of his hand.

"What do you want?" Khalid grumbled.

"We need to talk," Belial stated. "Now."

"Can't this wait until I'm finished eating?" Khalid asked pushing his food further away.

The smell of Belial's breath became more vulgar every second.

"No," replied Belial. His icy eyes reflected a coldness that would make the devil shiver. "I want what is due to me!"

"Keep your voice down," Hafeeza threatened.

She pushed her jacket backward revealing a small dagger in her belt.

Belial laughed then stopped as if a moment before he was not amused.

Sweat dampened Hafeeza's forehead. She placed her hand on the hilt of her knife.

Belial hissed at her; all tongue and teeth. He turned to Khalid.

"Bring the boy and our dealings will be no more," Belial affirmed.

"My brother is nonnegotiable. Pick someone else," Khalid said as he stood up towering over Belial like a giant over a baby.

Belial's shadow repositioned itself on the other side of Khalid.

"I fear we have a problem my friend," Belial fumed. "It seems that you are backing out of our bargain."

"My brother was never a part of our bargain. Pick someone else!" Khalid hissed as he pushed Belial out of his chair.

Belial looked up from the floor; a wide grin preternaturally stretching his face. Legs bent like a grasshopper's, he leapt up and wrapped his wiry legs around Khalid's waist punching him wildly in the face.

Belial's shadow attacked Khalid from behind raining blow upon blow upon his head.

Hafeeza fruitlessly grabbed at the shadow, her hands going through it like air. She redirected her attack towards Belial trying with all her strength to pull him from Khalid.

Belial's feet hit the floor in unison. He backhand slapped Hafeeza to the floor. He climbed on top of her and slapped her multiple times across the face then stood up and kicked her in the ribs as his shadow choked Khalid with its smoky arms.

"Come!" Belial commanded his shadow.

The shadow released Khalid and fell in line behind its master.

"I don't want to have this conversation again. Bring me the boy!" Belial growled as he turned on his heels and vanished from the cafeteria.

Hafeeza crawled to a table and pulled herself up into a chair.

"Are you okay?" she asked Khalid holding her side. A dark ring began to form around her eye.

"I will be," Khalid muttered, blood dripping from the corner of his mouth and out of his left nostril. His phone rang. He answered before realizing that it was a video call.

"What happened to you?" Uriel yelped, horrified by Khalid's battered face.

"I got into a little fight," he fumed.

"What does the other guy look like?" Uriel remarked. "Who did that to you?"

"My roommate," Khalid confessed.

"I'm on my way," said Uriel angrily.

"No! Stay away. You can't come here! Never come here. If you want to see me, I'll come to you," Khalid said. "I'm in a lot of trouble. I don't want you to get hurt."

"But..." Uriel lamented.

"But nothing! Don't come here! I will be alright. I can take care of myself!" Khalid replied. "Pray for me if it makes you feel better. Just don't come here. I promise that I will fix this on my own."

Uriel stared into the phone. Fear and anger quaked him.

"I'll talk to you later," Khalid said. "Love you bro," he said and disconnected the call. He placed his phone in his pocket.

"Is that who he wants?" Hafeeza asked; her top lip bubbling up and protruding from her face.

"Are you okay?" Khalid asked her, feeling terrible about her injuries on his behalf. "I'm sorry that you got mixed up in all this."

"I am here to serve you," she explained. "I will defend you unto death."

"I will make sure you won't have to. Belial will pay for this with his last breath," Khalid fumed.

He helped her to her feet and stormed out of the room.

LVII

"Dad, I need to talk to you," Uriel said tapping James on the shoulder.

James looked over his shoulder and invited his son to sit with him on the couch.

"What up man?" James asked. He turned down the television and gave Uriel his full attention.

"I'm worried. Khalid is in trouble," Uriel answered.

"What kinda trouble?" James asked, tension twisting his face.

"I'm not sure but when I called him on video phone he looked like he had been beaten up by a gang of people. His mouth and nose were bleeding. Bruises were on the sides of his face, and the neck of his t-shirt was ripped," Uriel lamented.

"What?" James sat up. "What he say happened?"

"He said that he had gotten into a fight with his roommate, but he was okay," Uriel answered.

"Did he look like he had any major injuries? Was he moving around okay?" James asked.

"No, he didn't look seriously injured and yes, he was moving around okay, but he was still beaten up pretty badly, Dad," Uriel replied. "We need to go see about him."

"Khalid can take care of hisself. He ain't no punk. If he say he good, Uriel, he good," James replied. He had no doubt that Khalid could handle himself and that he feared no one. A matter of fact, James felt that the blood on Khalid probably belonged to the victim.

"You don't understand. Lid's roommate isn't normal," Uriel exclaimed.

"Whatchu mean?" James inquired.

Unease tightened his chest. He was not interested in anything or anyone that wasn't normal.

"He's," Uriel paused at loss for words. "He's some kind of demon. You should see him dad. His skin is see-through. His eyes are clear and creepy. His breath smells like toilet chocolate and he has a shadow that moves on its own," Uriel explained.

"I don't got time for this," James griped.

"I'm serious!" Uriel belted.

"I'm sure you are," James grumbled. "How am I 'posed to help Lid with a demon? Am I 'posed to exorcise it? Am I 'posed to fight it?"

James stood up and dropped the TV remote on the couch.

"I'm not getting' involved in anything that boy got goin' on. I paid my dues. Lid is almost grown. If he told you he got it, then he got it!" James grumbled. "Let him handle his business and you stay away from that college campus. If I catch you even thinkin' about goin' over there Imma beat yo' ass. You hear me boy?" James pointed his thin finger at Uriel.

Uriel's face dropped. His father had never threatened him or cursed at him before. Uriel wanted to cry but figured he was too old to cry about hurt feelings.

"Do you hear me talkin' to you, Uriel?" James yelled.

"Yes sir," Uriel replied.

"I'm going to shoot some hoops. You wanna come?" James asked, the anger slowly draining from his face.

"No. I'm going to pray and meditate for a little while, then I may go visit Earth if that's okay," Uriel replied. He tried desperately to hide the hurt in his eyes.

"Cool," James said. "You like her, don't you?"

James smiled a fake smile as if the line of conversation would make Uriel forget the threat issued to him just moments before.

"Yeah," Uriel mumbled uncomfortably.

"She cute," James remarked.

Uriel nodded in agreement.

"Well, I betta head out. Talk to you lata," James said as he opened the front door and stepped outside.

Uriel turned to walk to his room when James called his name.

"Yes dad," Uriel answered.

"Don't mention Khalid to yo' mother. It would only worry her. Let her enjoy bein' happy 'bout Sky's recovery. She don't need to be stressed 'bout Lid. Especially when you and I both know that he can take care of hisself," he said and closed the door behind him.

Uriel stood staring at the closed door praying silently for God to order his footsteps.

LVIII

A billion stars twinkled in the sky. Venus couldn't believe that they were shining so brightly in a heavily illuminated city like Atlanta; seeing that much starlight was rare; eerie even. She drew closer to Khalid as they nestled on a blanket in the middle of the college lawn. Bags of half-eaten fast food littered the blanket. Shoes and socks sat next to them in a makeshift pyramid.

"You never told me what happened to your face," Venus said touching the side of his face with the back of her hand. Purple bruises freckled his face in fat blotches.

"You never told me how you were able to chill with me this late at night," Khalid remarked embarrassed by his appearance. Getting beat up was hard to swallow. Before that day in the cafeteria, he had never lost a fight. Venus tried to convince him to let her make up his face, but he refused. He would wear his bruises like a man.

"I snuck out of the house. It was easy. Jupiter sleeps like a dead man. Mars can't hear anything over his night noise machine. Earth was probably talking to your brother, and my mom and dad were getting it on to the sounds of Marvin Gaye. As long as I am back in my room before my dad wakes up for work, I'm good," Venus replied. "Now tell me, who rearranged your face?"

"You go hard," Khalid laughed.

"I keep it one hundred," Venus replied as she turned to face him. "Seriously, tell me what happened."

"My roommate attacked me in the cafeteria the other day," he admitted.

"What's going on with him? Tell me the truth. I want to know everything. Any fool with eyes can see that he ain't regular," Venus said.

"You won't believe me," Khalid replied, turning to face her. He leaned in and gave Venus an Eskimo kiss.

The nose tickle made her smile. She kissed his lips but pulled back before the smooch became too intense.

"Tell me," she pleaded. "Please."

Khalid told Venus everything. He told her about his roommate, Austin Underdue, being possessed by the demon Belial. Khalid told her how he had murdered people for the demon to possess, but all of the bodies were rejected. He told her about Turiel and his entrapment by Belial. He told her that he had killed Yvette and how Belial wanted Uriel. He told her what little he knew about Hafeeza and her desire to help him. Khalid poured out his deepest secrets to Venus and she listened silently without fear or judgement.

When he finished talking, they lay quietly for a tiny eternity before Khalid's uneasiness forced him to break the silence.

"What are you thinking?" he asked.

"I have an idea," Venus said rolling onto her side and propping herself up on her elbow.

"Shoot," said Khalid, eyebrow raised and intrigued by her response and lack of comment on his confessions. Venus didn't blink an eye when hearing about his indiscretions. It was quite baffling. How could his admissions not even garner a tiny response?

"I saw this documentary once about exorcising demons. It showed how people all over the world of different belief systems battled the same kinds of supernatural entities. Maybe we should get rid of your roommate that way. We both know that exorcism is possible," she commented. "Uriel performed one when he was a six-year-old kid. How hard could it be?"

Memories of Khalid's grandmother's death flooded him. Uriel had exorcised Turiel out of her. It was no easy feat and Uriel was not the average child. He had an anointing on him. Khalid was sure that neither he nor Venus had the same kind of power that Uriel possessed.

"Doesn't exorcism require some kind of faith base? You and I don't believe in anything but ourselves," Khalid laughed sadly.

"Not necessarily. We can look up some protection, boundary, and exorcism spells on the internet and try to trap him. Uriel might be a son of light, but you my love are the Prince of Darkness," Venus replied with a wicked smile on her face having no idea how true her statement may have been.

"You serious?" inquired Khalid.

"As a heart attack," she answered. "You down?"

"I'm down," Khalid agreed unable to keep himself from smiling. Venus was surely the one for him.

L|X

Stacks of homework covered Earth's full-sized bed and faux grass rug which blended perfectly with her floral-patterned bedspread and the hand painted enchanted forest on her wall. Vases of flowers and butterfly stickers on her ceiling made Uriel feel that Earth really internalized her name.

Open books lined with neon yellow highlighter and two open laptops sat back to back on the floor between Earth and Uriel. The sound of typing and hip hop filled the room as the teens completed their social studies project.

Earth looked up from her laptop.

"Are you hungry?" she asked. The sound of her stomach growling followed.

"Obviously you are," Uriel laughed. "I can eat. What do you have?"

"Everything," Earth replied. "My mother buys groceries like the apocalypse is coming. What do you have a taste for?"

"I'll eat anything," Uriel answered. "Surprise me."

Earth closed her laptop and exited the room. A quarter hour later she came back with two bowls of butternut squash ravioli, garlic bread, two small salads, and two glasses of pomegranate juice.

"Wow," Uriel exclaimed. "I thought you were coming back with bologna sandwiches."

"I don't eat bologna," Earth responded with an air of disgust.

Uriel laughed and accepted the food.

"Thank you. It smells really good," he complimented.

The two ate quietly. When they finished, Earth piled their dishes upon a tray and returned them to the kitchen. She came back and began typing on her laptop.

"Can we talk?" Uriel asked.

"Sure," Earth said looking up from her computer.

"I'm worried about my brother," Uriel confessed. "When I talked to him last, his face was battered and bruised. He looked pretty bad."

"What happened?" Earth asked.

Jupiter walked into her open bedroom door; his red hair hanging long at the top and faded on the sides. He had been walking down the hall when he heard what Uriel said.

"Is he okay?" Jupiter asked.

He and Khalid had a pretty cool relationship. They considered each other close associates. They weren't close like Khalid and Venus, but Jupiter and Khalid talked from time to time and chilled out when he came home. Jupiter wanted to know if he needed to take a visit to Khalid's school to help him handle some business.

"I don't know," Uriel admitted. "He said that he was, but he looked pretty bad."

"What did your pops say?" Jupiter asked leaning against the doorpost. His skinny legs looked like pale pencils dangling from his basketball shorts.

"He said that Lid could take care of himself and to stay out of it," replied Uriel. "If dad would have seen him, he wouldn't have been so nonchalant about the situation."

"Does your mom know?" Jupiter asked a little annoyed by James's reaction to Khalid's situation. Secretly, James annoyed Jupiter in general. He hated how James always tried to avoid situations instead of facing things head on.

"No. Dad told me not to tell her," said Uriel.

Jupiter huffed. He left Earth's room and headed straight to his mother's. He knocked on the door.

"Come in," Sky called.

Jupiter opened the door.

Sky sat on her fainting couch typing on her laptop. He was happy to see that she was writing again. Her thick and shiny scarlet hair was beginning to grow again. Her skin looked vibrant and healthy. Her skeletal form had picked up a tiny amount of weight, so she looked a lot less emaciated. She was beautiful again. It was amazing how she had transformed so quickly. Jupiter smiled for a moment then remembered why he was there.

"Uriel told me that Khalid had gotten into a fight and was beaten pretty badly," Jupiter explained. "Uriel told James about it, and James told him not to worry about it. Auntie Sadie doesn't know. I'm telling you in case Khalid might be in real trouble."

"Thanks, baby," Sky replied as she put down her laptop and picked up her cell phone.

LX

"Are you sure this is going to work?" Khalid whispered as he spread a circle of salt around Belial's bed as he slept. He was happy that he had done the first half of the circle when Belial was out of the room. Now all he had to do was to ensure the circle was complete.

"It should," Venus whispered back as she lined Khalid's bed with crystals, mojo bags, various powders, and cultic seals. "I researched the techniques of Wiccans, Voodoo, Yoruba, and Native American and Indian shamans. I figure if we use a bit of everything, something should work."

Khalid shook his head. A sense of impending doom filled him. He couldn't believe he allowed his admiration for Venus to get him in such a stupid situation.

Venus hung a charm around her neck and one around Khalid's.

"Are you ready?" she asked.

Khalid nodded.

Venus cleared her throat, lit a bundle of sage, and began to hum loudly.

Belial opened his eyes and sat up on his bed. His shadow sat beside him.

Khalid drew a pentagram on the floor. He then wrote Belial's name down on a piece of parchment paper and lit a black candle.

He took the paper and traced the pentagram as he said, "I banish you Belial from this space. You have no power over us. I cast you back into the darkness where you belong."

Belial began to laugh hysterically until Khalid lit the paper and tossed it into a small cauldron to burn.

Belial cried out in pain. He fell backward on his bed.

"It's working!" Venus exclaimed.

Belial sprang up and began to laugh hysterically again.

"You think an amateur spell can banish me?" he growled.

He sprang up from his bed but was stopped by an invisible force. His foot could not cross the line of salt. Fuming, he sat back down.

Venus pulled a few sheets of paper from her purse and began to read off them. With each spell she uttered, Belial became angrier and angrier.

"When I get free, I'm going to skin her alive," he threatened, his eyes narrowing like a serpent's. "I'm going to fry her skin and eat it like pork rinds."

"I bind you from all sides. I bind you day and night. I bind you from doing harm to us or to our families. I bind you Belial! As above, so below. So, mote it be!" Venus yelled as she braided yarn around one of Belial's ancient ink pens. She placed the items in a jar and twisted the lid tight.

Belial's arms and legs twisted into a fleshly knot causing him to fall back upon his bed.

"Look!" Venus exclaimed grabbing hold of Khalid's arm. "I bound him!" she jumped up and down excitedly. She dropped the jar and it shattered.

Belial's limbs loosened, and he sprang up hissing with his tongue dripping with curses.

Khalid shook his head in disbelief. They almost had him. Now they were back to square one.

"You can't hold me like this forever," Belial growled. He pulled himself on hands and feet like a frog ready to leap.

"I have a spell to power Chango!" Venus cried. The look in Belial's eyes became more mincing by the second. "I also have a few blood magic spells," she offered.

"You better stop while you are ahead," Belial warned. "You may mess around and invite some of my friends into the room."

Turiel's eyes stretched wide. His mouth opened but there was no sound. Khalid knew that his father was trying to warn them. It was time to take heed.

Venus pulled out a pocket knife and pressed it into her palm.

"No," Khalid yelled. "Don't do that."

"Yeah! Don't do that!" Belial concurred. He sat down and crossed his legs. His face softened. "I have a bargain for you. If you make her leave now, I promise I won't kill her, and I will forget this whole asinine episode. If you keep me here a minute longer, I will cut her into bite sized pieces as I wear your brother as a meat suit."

There was something in Belial's eyes that Khalid had never seen before; something evil and diabolical to a degree his mind could not comprehend. He knew that Belial wasn't just tossing out empty threats. He meant what he said. The demon would kill Venus and Uriel if they did not stop with the exorcism spells. The horrified look in Turiel's eyes verified Khalid's postulation.

"Get out of here!" Khalid said to Venus. "Go home and never come back here. I will visit you from now on."

"But..." Venus started.

"Now!" Khalid thundered.

"We can do this! We can bind him!" Venus exclaimed. "He's just trying to scare us. If he could kill me, he would have already!"

Khalid didn't want to take a chance on the lives of his love ones.

"Get out!" he yelled knocking her next batch of spell ingredients from her hand. His eyes blacked out.

Venus sprinted from the room and never looked back.

"Wise choice," Belial said. "Now, break the salt circle."

"Not until Venus is home safely," Khalid replied feeling utterly defeated and idiotic. If he was alone he would weep with frustration, but he was not alone and would never give Belial the pleasure of seeing him cry.

"At least pass me my book," Belial said with a crooked smile on his face.

Khalid threw Belial the book that was on his nightstand. It landed short of the salt circle.

Khalid let out a sigh of relief and Belial let out a sigh of disappointment. He picked up the book from the foot of his bed.

"I have to give it to you. Your girlfriend is dedicated and brave. She's a keeper," Belial mumbled as he leaned back and found the page where he had left off.

LXII

"Why didn't you tell me that Khalid had gotten into a fight?" Sadie yelled.

James sat at the kitchen table looking at her like she had two heads.

"Answer me!" she yelled.

"The boy can take care of hisself. He don't need his mama runnin' to his rescue," James snapped as he sat with his hands finger locked.

"That doesn't give you the right to keep information from me and it sure as hell doesn't give you the right to tell our son not to tell me about his brother!" she thundered as she paced the floor in front of him.

"Look, I didn't want to worry you. Lid was in a minor scrape. He a'ight," James replied coolly. "You need to calm down."

"Don't tell me to calm down! I video phoned Khalid and he looked like he had been run over by a car!" she retorted.

"You win some. You lose some," James said unaffected by Sadie's emotional tirade.

"You don't care, do you? You don't care what happens to our son!" Sadie screamed.

"Your son," James mumbled under his breath.

"What did you say?" Sadie asked, her hands on her hips and her neck bend downward so that she can catch his words again.

James said nothing.

"Wow," Sadie exclaimed.

"I don't wanna fight, Sadie. Things been good between us. Just let it go," James requested. "You makin' this bigger than it need to be."

" James, you're not making it big enough! Did you see Khalid's face?" Sadie asked.

"Nope," James replied looking upward to the side.

Sadie pulled her phone out of her pants pocket and pulled up a screenshot of Khalid's face.

"Look!" she thrusted the phone into James's face. "You think this is not a big deal?"

James saw Khalid's purple and blue face. His lips were swollen, and he had a black eye and broken skin. He didn't know Khalid was beaten that badly. Guilt filled James, but truth be told, he still didn't want Sadie and Uriel to get involved.

"I'm sorry," James lied. "I didn't know it was that bad. It was not my intention to keep things from you. I just didn't want you to worry."

Sadie looked at him. If she had the nerve, she would backhand slap him out of his seat, but she knew violence was never the answer. Besides, she wasn't sure if he would hit her back off reflex alone. She crossed her arms to curb the desire to strike out.

"I'm sorry, baby," James repeated.

The look in his eyes did not match what came out of his mouth. Sadie knew her husband well. He was lying through his teeth. She put the phone back into her pocket and pulled a chair and sat across from her husband.

James placed his hand upon hers.

"You forgive me?" James asked.

He kissed her knuckles and prayed silently that they could end their discussion, so he could leave to play basketball with Luis and Forrest. Last thing he wanted to do on a free weekend was to argue with Sadie. Arguing with Sadie was an all-day ordeal.

"Only if you promise not to keep things from me," Sadie said. "If you want our marriage to remain close, we have to be able to trust each other and to talk to each other."

"I promise," he lied again.

He had no intentions of telling her about anything that had to do with Khalid's trouble. The boy was in college. As far as James was concerned, Khalid was a grown man, and James was not in the business of solving personal problems for adults.

"I also want you to call Khalid and talk to him. Try to find out what went down. He told Uriel it was a fight with his roommate. He wouldn't tell me anything. I think it was more than that. Venus was close-lipped about it when Sky asked her," Sadie said.

"I'll call 'em," James replied getting up from the table. He kissed Sadie on the cheek and said, "I gotta go. The boys are waiting on me. I'll be back in time for dinner."

"Have fun," Sadie mumbled still awfully angry about the entire situation. She decided to take her therapist's advice and just let it go.

LXIII

The bell rang for the high school students to go to second period. The halls flooded with teens as they transitioned from class to class. Earth made her way down the science hall when Uriel pulled her into an empty lab room.

"What's going on?" Earth asked taken aback by Uriel's uncharacteristic aggression.

"I need to go see my brother. I fell asleep in class and had an awful dream. He's in trouble. I have to go," Uriel said.

"When?" Earth asked freeing her arm from his grasp.

"Now! Come with me?" Uriel asked, his eyes searching hers.

"Okay," Earth agreed. "How will we get there?"

"The train," Uriel answered. "Follow me," he requested as he led her out of the back door of the lab. They ran across campus, down the street to the bus stop. The bus arrived in minutes. The fourteen-year old's boarded and rode to the nearest train station. They boarded the train and exited blocks away from Khalid's college campus.

"What do you plan to do?" Earth asked nervously as she followed awkwardly behind him. She had never skipped school before. She couldn't help but to think about all the trouble she would be in if her parents found out.

"Help," Uriel answered.

He reached back and grabbed her hand, so she could keep pace with him as he moved swiftly towards Khalid's residential building.

Luckily when they arrived, the Resident Assistant was away from his desk, so they were able to slip past and head straight into the elevator. Earth was relieved that they didn't have to take the stairs. She was tired from Uriel pulling her down the street.

Uriel banged on Khalid's dorm room door so hard that the students in the hallway paused and took notice. The door shook under the force of his fist. The door swung open and Belial stood pleasantly surprised to see Uriel.

"Where is my brother?" Uriel yelled, fist balled and chest heaving.

"I don't know, but you are welcome to come in and wait," Belial invited with a palm wave.

"No," Earth yelped, pulling his arm. "We can come back."

Uriel looked at her then back to Belial. His spirit told him to listen to her, but his rage and hunger for vengeance told him to wait for his brother.

"We'll wait," Uriel belted as he pushed past Belial; knocking him into the door.

Belial regained his footing and closed the door behind them.

"When do you expect him back?" Earth asked, her voice trembling so hard that it sounded like she was speaking through a fan.

Belial lifted and dropped his shoulders.

Uriel and Earth took a seat on Khalid's bed as Belial walked over to his desk and opened his antique box. He pulled out an ancient scroll which he stretched out to full length. He began to read the primordial script.

The two children sat confused by the foreign words.

Belial continued to read.

Uriel unconsciously stood up. His legs moved without his permission and took one step in front of the other until he was standing directly in front of Belial. Belial's shadow stood behind Uriel making him the meat in the middle of a demon sandwich.

"Help!" Uriel cried as Belial laid his hand upon Uriel's head.

Earth jumped up but was knocked unconscious by the shadow's swift movement which caused her to fall and hit the side of her head on Khalid's desk.

"Earth!" Uriel cried.

She said nothing as she lay sprawled across the floor like a rag doll. Blood leaked from a cut on her temple.

Uriel screamed.

"Shush now! You don't want to bring attention to this room," Belial coaxed. He turned back to his scroll and continued his incantation.

Fire and ice rushed through Uriel's system as Belial chanted. Austin Underdue's body hit the floor as a dark cloud left his mouth. The cloud tried to force itself into Uriel's mouth, but Uriel refused to open his jaws. Tears rushed down his face as he fought against the invading spirit. Uriel prayed in his heart for deliverance to come.

The door swung open and Khalid stepped into the room. At once, the cloud reentered Austin Underdue's body and Belial stood up.

"Get away from him!" Khalid screamed as he rushed to his brother's aid. He knocked Uriel to the side and landed a blow across Belial's face. The demon fell backward.

"Get out of here!" Khalid yelled at Uriel. "Get out now! I told you to never come back here!"

Uriel picked up Earth from the floor and cradled her in his arms. He carried her from the room as Khalid and Belial battled behind him.

Uriel made it out of the building when he heard a loud crash and saw Belial falling from the dorm room window. The demon hit the ground with a huge thump. Khalid came running into the courtyard straight to the fallen Belial.

Khalid punched Belial until his thin pale skin lay in threads. The demon bit into Khalid's arm which sent him wailing backward, then the demon pounced upon him and began to bite into Khalid's chest like a hyena into a crippled giraffe.

Earth regained consciousness and Uriel sat her upon the dorm steps.

"Stop!" Uriel cried rushing towards the fight. Before he could reach his brother, Hafeeza blocked his path.

"Go see about your friend," she said. "I will help him.

She pulled a carved stick from her coat and ran top speed towards Belial. She struck him in the back of the head sending him flying across the ground. Hafeeza jabbed the demon over and over until he lay still. She turned back to see about Khalid; dropping her stick to tend to his wounds. She removed his shirt and made a tourniquet for his bleeding arm.

"Thank you," Khalid whispered.

"You're..." Hafeeza started when she was pulled backward by her hair. She frantically grabbed at her hair trying to wrench it out of Belial's fingers. He pulled her across the grass, her legs kicking wildly. He dragged her past her stick. She grabbed it and pushed the stick over her head; jabbing the demon in the stomach causing him to tumble backward. The carvings on her staff glowed a bright blue. She twirled it above her head displaying her skill and rushed towards the fallen demon. Aiming it at his heart, she thrust the stick forward, but Belial's shadow caught the end of the staff from behind Hafeeza and snatched it from the air. The glowing stick blazed causing the shadow to drop it. Before Hafeeza could pick it up, Belial was upon her. He grabbed her by the hair again, this time wrapping it around her hands so tight that blood began to drip from her scalp.

Belial pulled her neck to the side and ripped her throat out with his teeth. He spit her flesh to the ground and dropped her dead body beside it.

A hooded woman slipped through the crowd and picked up the staff, then was gone as quickly as she came.

LX|V

Sadie washed the last dish from the night before and decided to sit down to enjoy a glass of iced tea. She wanted to hear music but was too lazy to go get the portable speaker. James wanted to place a radio in the kitchen, but kitchen radios gave Sadie the worst form of déjà vu. They reminded her of her first encounter with Turiel and she needed no reminder of that; ever. Sadie picked up a crossword puzzle and began to scribble words onto the paper when her cell phone buzzed on the kitchen counter.

"Hello," Sadie answered finishing a word and reading the next clue.

"May I speak to Mrs. Tucker?" a voice asked through Sadie's cell phone. The caller ID read that the call was from Uriel's high school.

"This is she. How may I help you?" Sadie asked putting her glass of iced tea on the counter. It was rare that she received phone calls from the school. Something must have been amiss.

"This is Mrs. Pauline McGree. I'm the Attendance Supervisor. Uriel Tucker left school early today. Are you aware of this?" Mrs. McGree said; her voice aged and crackly.

"No," Sadie replied. "I did not give Uriel permission to leave nor did his father."

" A teacher saw him, and a young lady get on the bus about an hour ago. The school officer tried to catch them, but they were gone before he got to them," Mrs. McGree said.

"Thank you for notifying me," Sadie replied. "I will take care of it."

"Our school takes attendance and the safety of our students very seriously..." Ms. McGree droned.

"I said I will take care of it!" Sadie snapped cutting Mrs. McGree off. "Thanks again for calling," Sadie said before hanging up the phone. Sadie called James at work.

"Hey, baby," James answered. "I'm in the middle of a meeting." James smiled at the two people sitting in front of his desk. "Can I call you back?"

"Uriel left school. I think he took Earth with him!" Sadie cried. "Why would he do that?"

"He loves his brother. I'll meet you at Khalid's school. I'm leaving now," James said standing up and grabbing his jacket from the back of his chair. "Love you," he said before hanging up his office phone.

"We'll have to reschedule. Make an appointment with my assistant," James said and rushed out of the door before his colleagues could respond.

Sadie grabbed her keys and ran barefoot to her car. She started the car up and sped off leaving her front door wide open.

One of her neighbors saw it and closed it for her.

While waiting at a red light, Sadie texted a message to Sky asking her to check on Earth because she may have skipped school with Uriel.

Sadie and James pulled into the university parking lot at the same time. They parked next to each other in the back parking lot of the school. Sadie, barefoot and wearing nothing but yoga pants and a crop top, sprinted across the yard towards Khalid's dorm. James was on her heels. Both were stopped by a large crowd gasping, crying, screaming, and recording with their cell phones. The couple pushed their way through to see what all the commotion was about.

"No!" Sadie screamed as she saw her first-born son's skin being cut into shreds by the nails of Belial and her younger son praying out loud like a crazed religious zealot.

Khalid, blinded by blood and sweat, broke free of Belial's grasp. He picked up a large stone and slammed it into the side of Belial's head knocking him to the ground. Khalid raised the stone above his head as Belial's long fingers wrapped around Khalid's neck. As the stone crushed Belial's skull, Khalid's neck broke with a loud crack. Khalid fell to Belial's side; his neck twisted like a wrung towel.

Belial left Austin Underdue's dead body in a loud shriek. The demon ascended into the air as a dark cloud then dissolved into nothing. His shadow absorbed into Khalid's cooling flesh. The demon was gone.

"No!" Sadie cried as she ran to her son. She cradled his dead body as she screamed to the top of her lungs.

LXV

A bright light flooded Khalid's dorm room. Turiel's chains dropped to the floor and his dangling wing melted into his skin until he was made whole again. The cord around Turiel's neck snapped and fell to the floor. He let out an ear-piercing cry that rang out like a ram's horn. It filled the dorm, bursting windows on every floor. Screaming students ran from the building in droves.

The scream poured out of the window causing the people outside to fall to their knees holding their ears. In a flash of white light, Turiel flew out of the dorm room window.

When the sound lifted, Sadie refocused her attention on her oldest son.

"My baby!" Sadie cried. "My baby!" she rocked Khalid as her husband and younger son gathered around her.

The crowd quieted and watched on as the family lamented the death of their kin.

"Why?" Sadie screamed hysterically as James tried to calm her.

Uriel and Earth wept without ceasing.

The sound of police sirens, fire trucks, and ambulances echoed in the background.

The students filed away one by one full of grief and disbelief. Their campus idol had fallen in the strangest battle their human eyes had ever witnessed. Those who recorded the fight looked at their phones to discover recordings of soundless black. The crowd parted like the red sea to let the police and ambulance through.

Sadie clung to her son, tears casting the world in a confusing blur. The EMTs tried to pry Khalid's body free of her arms but she refused to release him.

James rained kisses and tears upon her head.

"Let 'em go," James coaxed. "Let 'em go."

"I can't," she wailed as she kissed Khalid's face. She closed his eyes and kissed his eyelids.

"You have to. He's gone," James said. Tears ran down his face. Despite everything, he loved his son and seeing his twisted body, head dangling from his broken neck, in his mother's arms made James want to crawl under a rock and die.

Uriel, in tears and sobbing uncontrollably, prayed over his brother's dead body, but Khalid remained unmoving.

"Stop," James told Uriel. "He is with God now. We have to comfort your mother."

Uriel stopped praying, but continued weeping. It felt as if the world was falling down. His brother completed him. There was no way life could continue without Khalid.

Sadie unwrapped her arms from around her first-born son and wrapped them around her husband.

The EMTs lifted Khalid's bloody body onto a stretcher. His head dangled from his neck like a ball on a string. The EMTs took his vitals and verified his death. As one of the EMTs began to pull a sheet over Khalil's head, Turiel flew overhead casting a shadow upon them all.

All eyes went upward staring at what they perceived as a huge bird.

Sadie knew better. She knew those wings and that smell anywhere. She clutched James's arms and let out a faint cry.

In an instant, Turiel transformed into a ray of light and pierced the chest of Khalid. The angel flew into the sun as the people fell prostrate.

One by one the people got up from the ground dazed, confused, and semi-blinded by the light.

Sadie resumed her crying as James and the others stood awestruck at what they thought they had seen.

An EMT worker began to pull the sheet over Khalid's head. The man froze as the flesh of Khalid's neck began to move around like a hoard of insets were under his skin. His neck straightened and untwisted itself like an unwinding toy.

Khalid inhaled loudly and opened his eyes.